"You look great, by the way. Really, really great."

Now *she* crossed her arms over her chest. "Are you paid to say that?"

"You can see for yourself that you look like the woman you want to turn into, Ginger."

"Who—" she began, then bit her lip and glanced down.

Who died and left you king? was what she was going to say. "Sorry," she said. "Now I'm being bossy. And a jerk."

"You're not a jerk. I'd rather you spoke your mind than didn't."

"But I don't agree with you."

"At least I know how you feel. And getting other points of view is good, especially from people you respect."

She put her hands on her curvy hips. "Would you respect me if I didn't look like a newscaster on her day off?"

He laughed. "Yes. Because you tell it like you see it. And you're smart. It's a good combo."

"Stop making it hard for me to want to conk you on the head with a banana."

* * *

THE WYOMING MULTIPLES:
Lots of babies, lots of love

Dear Reader,

With her heavy makeup, bleached-blond big hair, skimpy clothes and job as a barmaid, twenty-four-year-old Ginger O'Leary gets whispered about and put down. She's used to that. Ginger is comfortable in her own skin and likes who she is. But when she discovers she's pregnant and the baby's rich father threatens to fight for custody because of how she looks, talks and acts, Ginger will do anything to keep her baby. Even if it means changing *everything* about herself.

So when she enrolls at Madame Davenport's School of Etiquette in Wedlock Creek, Wyoming, she expects to become a person deemed worthy of being a mother. But with her teacher's handsome godson, businessman James Gallagher, in her corner, Ginger and James both may discover more than they ever expected about acceptance, parenthood and love.

I hope you enjoy Ginger and James's love story! I love to hear from readers. Feel free to visit my website and write me at melissasenate@yahoo.com.

Warmest regards,

Melissa Senate

To Keep Her Baby

Melissa Senate

HARLEQUIN® SPECIAL EDITION

Recycling programs
for this product may
not exist in your area.

ISBN-13: 978-1-335-57378-0

To Keep Her Baby

Copyright © 2019 by Melissa Senate

All rights reserved. Except for use in any review, the reproduction or
utilization of this work in whole or in part in any form by any electronic,
mechanical or other means, now known or hereafter invented, including
xerography, photocopying and recording, or in any information storage
or retrieval system, is forbidden without the written permission of the
publisher, Harlequin Enterprises Limited, 22 Adelaide St. West, 40th Floor,
Toronto, Ontario M5H 4E3, Canada.

This is a work of fiction. Names, characters, places and incidents are
either the product of the author's imagination or are used fictitiously,
and any resemblance to actual persons, living or dead, business
establishments, events or locales is entirely coincidental.

This edition published by arrangement with Harlequin Books S.A.

For questions and comments about the quality of this book,
please contact us at CustomerService@Harlequin.com.

® and TM are trademarks of Harlequin Enterprises Limited or its
corporate affiliates. Trademarks indicated with ® are registered in the
United States Patent and Trademark Office, the Canadian Intellectual
Property Office and in other countries.

Printed in U.S.A.

Melissa Senate has written many novels for Harlequin and other publishers, including her debut, *See Jane Date*, which was made into a TV movie. She also wrote seven books for Harlequin's Special Edition line under the pen name Meg Maxwell. Her novels have been published in over twenty-five countries. Melissa lives on the coast of Maine with her teenage son; their rescue shepherd mix, Flash; and a lap cat named Cleo. For more information, please visit her website, melissasenate.com.

Books by Melissa Senate

Harlequin Special Edition

The Wyoming Multiples

The Baby Switch!
Detective Barelli's Legendary Triplets
Wyoming Christmas Surprise

Furever Yours

A New Leash on Love

Hurley's Homestyle Kitchen (as Meg Maxwell)

A Cowboy in the Kitchen
The Detective's 8 lb, 10 oz Surprise
The Cowboy's Big Family Tree
The Cook's Secret Ingredient
Charm School for Cowboys
Santa's Seven-Day Baby Tutorial

Montana Mavericks: The Lonelyhearts Ranch

The Maverick's Baby-in-Waiting

Visit the Author Profile page
at Harlequin.com for more titles.

For my mother, with love.

Chapter One

"Miss O'Leary, please describe your goals if accepted as a pupil of Madame Davenport's School of Etiquette," Larilla Davenport said from behind her desk.

"Just look at me," Ginger blurted out as she stood up. Her low-cut hot-pink tank top, size extra, extra small, showed the lacy tops of her leopard-print push-up bra. *Babe* was written in rhinestones across her ample chest. Her ruffled miniskirt, which came to an end just past her rear, was also extra small. Big was her platinum blond hair in "beachy waves" to her waist. Four-inch stilettos, a bunch of cheap bracelets and heavy makeup completed her usual daytime look.

The fiftysomething woman sitting across from her—so spiffy in an ice-blue sheath dress and matching jacket, her dark hair pulled back in one of those elegant buns at her nape—looked Ginger up and down. Yeah, she was used to that.

"My dear," Madame Davenport said, "if you were just interested in changing your look, you could wash your face and buy a few new outfits. So why are you *really* interested in enrolling in my course?"

Because of last night. And this morning. Which felt like eons ago but had just been hours before. It started with the pregnancy test. The red plus sign appearing in the little window. Racing back to Walgreens for another test, which Ginger had taken in the bathroom at Busty's, the "exotic dance saloon" where she worked as a waitress. Another plus sign. She was pregnant. Her, Ginger O'Leary. Someone's mother?

The thought of it had knocked around in her head during her shift last night, serving the tap of the day and shots to leering customers. *I'm pregnant?* she'd kept thinking, setting down baskets of breaded mozzarella sticks and plates of loaded nachos on tables. Me?

Ginger O'Leary had lost her virginity at fifteen. She was now twenty-four. That was nine years of sex with guys who she'd been naive about, but she'd always been careful, keeping several boxes of condoms in her bedroom and car, and always a few packets in her purse. This time though, the condom had broken, and the man who'd had it on had muttered expletives, grabbed his clothes and run out of her apartment.

For the past year, he'd been coming into Busty's twice a week and always left with a different waitress each time. He was one of the richies. There were the richies and the poors, per the female staff. The richies were the ones who looked—key word *looked*—like gentlemen who left ten-dollar tips. The poors were jerks who said stuff like "Here's your tip—flash me and I'll leave you a buck." Busty's was a real quality operation.

Anyway, Alden Arlington, the father of her baby, hadn't come in last night but she'd seen him this morning, heading into Java Jamboree with a woman. She'd trailed him into the café and asked if she could talk to him, and he'd said, "I'm surprised you get up before noon."

Normally she didn't. But this wasn't a normal day. Like she could sleep.

She told him it was super important, and finally, the woman at his table gave her a dirty look and said she'd go order their lattes and scones.

Ginger sat down in the woman's seat. "I thought you should know I'm pregnant," she whispered to him. "I just found out yesterday."

"Uh, congratulations?" Alden said. God, he was good-looking. All that movie-star blond hair, the green eyes. The expensive suit. He looked like a young Brad Pitt. Of course, being gorgeous and nicely dressed didn't make him a nice guy. He'd avoided Busty's for a good two weeks after the broken-condom incident, then started coming back in a couple nights a week again and ignoring her, leaving with other women. Whatevs. She hadn't been hanging her hopes on him as a boyfriend, but he didn't have to treat her like she wasn't worth a hello.

"It's yours," she said.

He laughed. "Sure it is, honey. You probably sleep

with more men in a week than there are in here right now."

Ginger actually gasped, which surprised her. She wasn't the gasping type. People said a lot of crap to her. But she didn't actually sleep around. She'd liked Alden, had hoped he'd notice her, and he had. Before he'd shown his true colors, she'd had all these fantasies that he'd fall for her and carry her out of Busty's like Richard Gere had swooped Debra Winger out of the factory in that movie *An Officer and a Gentleman.*

"Find some idiot to pin it on," he said. "I'm a little too smart for that."

The woman came back to the table just then with coffee drinks and plates, and sat down on the other side of Alden, sipping her latte. "Listen to me, sweetie," she said, staring at Ginger with ice-cold eyes. "You're saying it's my brother's baby? Fine. A DNA test will prove you're lying. On the off chance you're not? Expect a custody battle since you're not exactly fit to be a mother."

"What's that supposed to mean?" Ginger snapped, hands on her hips.

"Look at you," she said, waving her hand up and down.

"It's not mine, so don't even waste your breath on this lowlife," Alden said to his sister, picking up his drink.

Ginger grabbed the scone and threw it at him. It hit him on his tie and bounced on the table, then landed on the floor. "Screw you."

"That's battery," the sister said, pointing a manicured finger. "We could have her charged."

Cursing herself for her temper and impulsiveness, a

lick of fear traveled up her spine. She'd rushed out, practically running all the way back to Busty's and trying to calm down in the very bathroom stall where she'd taken the pregnancy test.

"My goodness," Larilla Davenport said, jerking Ginger out of the memory.

Had Ginger meant to say word for word what happened? Out loud? Maybe not. But hey, one thing you could say about Ginger O'Leary was that she told the truth.

Ginger sat up straight and looked Madame Davenport in the eyes. "You asked me what my goals are if I get accepted as a student here. All I want is to be a good mother to this baby." She looked down at her still-flat belly, then shook her head at the *Babe* across her big chest, which was natural, by the way, and not enhanced—except by the push-up bra. "*Babe* is now about the baby, Madame Davenport. Not me. I'm going to be someone's mother. I have to change—and not just how I look. Everything about me. How I talk, act, think. I need to become proper. I need to become the kind of person who doesn't get called a lowlife, you know? Someone who doesn't throw baked goods at people out of anger. Because Alden could take the baby away. I need to become the kind of person who won't get her baby taken away."

Tears poked at her eyes, and she slashed a hand underneath each. "Madame Davenport, if I'm going to raise my baby right, I need to *be* right. And if I ever hope to find a good man to be a father to my baby, I have to become the type of woman a good man brings home to meet the folks."

Madame stared at her for a moment, then jotted something down in the electronic tablet on the ornate polished desk. "I see. How did you hear of my etiquette school, Ms. O'Leary?"

"Well, my boss at Busty's is this really kick-ass lady. She pulled herself up from nothing. I asked her how she accomplished that, and she said she'd spent all her savings a few years back to go to etiquette school in Wedlock Creek. Coco told me the course teaches everything from how to act, dress, order in a restaurant, what not to say, what *to* say—all that. So I told her I had to quit, got in my car and drove three hours from Jackson."

Madame Davenport smiled. "Ah, Coco. I remember her. I admired her spunk."

Ginger too. "Problem is, I can't exactly afford five minutes of one class, forget about the three-week session." Ginger had $212 to her name. She glanced around at the office, full of antiques and oil paintings on the walls. The beautiful Queen Anne–style house was like a castle—surely Madame Davenport needed another cleaning person or prep cook. "I'll do any job in exchange for the etiquette course. Anything. I'll scrub all the toilets till they sparkle."

Madame Davenport eyed Ginger and snapped the cover of the tablet closed. "My dear, you will not scrub anything but yourself into the person you want to be. You are hereby enrolled in the three-week session that starts tomorrow. On scholarship."

For the second time ever, Ginger O'Leary gasped.

* * *

Have a few moments to help with a new pupil assessment?

James Gallagher read the text from his godmother and groaned. He used to help out at Larilla's etiquette school quite a bit, playing the role of "upstanding young man in the community" so that Larilla could assess how students acted around the opposite sex and practice their newfound skills in conversation. Larilla had a list of men of all ages who loved helping out at the school, but all her favorites must be unavailable today.

The last time he helped with an assessment was last year, in the final days of Ava Guthrie's course. He'd watched Ava transform from a "country girl," as she'd called herself, into a "lady," and he'd given her top scores in the final assessment. She'd hooked *him*, hadn't she? A "well-educated businessman," twenty-eight-year-old James Gallagher was one of Wedlock Creek's "hottest catches," per a ridiculous article in the *Wedlock Creek Gazette* that his sisters loved to tease him about. Last year, he'd even been thinking about getting himself removed from the eligible-bachelor list because he'd found his Ms. Right.

But Ava Guthrie had played him for the fool he was. After she'd gotten what she wanted—to be the kind of woman who'd attract a man like him—the grifter had gone for the kill, leaving town and taking James's ability to trust. She'd sped off in the shiny new Fiat he'd bought her. Like an idiot.

After that fiasco, his godmother had kindly stopped

asking him to help. Larilla knew he'd do anything for her, just as she would do anything for him. His parents and grandparents on both sides were long gone, and Larilla was all he had left of his mother's side of the family. On his dad's side he had the five half siblings he'd raised since his father's and stepmother's deaths seven years ago. Larilla had always been his rock. If she asked a favor, he was damn well going to grant it. Besides, a month and a week from now, he'd be in Paris, France, the start of his long-awaited summer sabbatical trip around the world. He wouldn't be able to help Larilla with anything, and he owed her.

Be right over, he typed back.

Wonderful! We're in the dining room.

It was just after six, but Larilla structured her course so that she met with a few students individually throughout the day and held group sessions twice daily. She always assessed new students over a private meal so that she could see how they conducted themselves at the table.

Larilla's home, which housed the etiquette school, was just a few minutes' drive from his place. He left his room, the converted attic bedroom, and headed down the steep steps of the big house his father had bought when he'd married James's stepmother twenty-two years ago. None of his siblings were home, no surprise there. The quints were twenty-one now, and two—his brothers— had left town for their dream jobs, one involving a prosperous ranch and the other as a sous chef in a five-star hotel in Cheyenne. Two of his sisters worked as assistants to Larilla, wanting to learn the business, which pleased his godmother to no end, and then there was Josie, who was generally responsible for his carrying three rolls of Tums wherever he went. *"You* are responsible for your reaction to me, James, so don't blame the heartburn on me!" Josie had bellowed a time or two.

He passed his dad and stepmother's old master bedroom in the huge house. None of the Gallagher siblings had felt right about moving in there, including him. They used it as a family room so that they'd always feel their dad and Kerry with them when they were watching movies or TV, or having family meetings about who the slob who couldn't cap the toothpaste or wipe up the spills on the kitchen counter was.

James couldn't believe it had been seven years since he'd lost his parents. Or that he'd actually done it—seen the siblings through the throes of raging adolescence at thirteen to twenty-one-year-olds living their lives. He'd put his own life on hold to raise them, but come a month from now, James was hitting the road—the skies, actually—for a global summer trip of no responsibility to anyone but himself. He'd eat the best pasta in the universe in Italy. Amazing bread and cheese in France. Paella, a favorite of his, in Spain. Sushi and real ramen in Japan. He'd go on safari in Africa. Swim the coral reefs in Australia. He'd even try to learn to meditate in India, not that he could imagine relaxing to that degree.

He was going to see the world—without a care. He. Could. Not. Wait.

He drove over to Larilla's blush-colored Queen

Anne, the sight of which never failed to make him smile. With its three-story octagonal tower and ornate wraparound veranda, the house *looked* like an etiquette school. A sign noting Madame Davenport's School of Etiquette hung from the side of the porch, where Larilla's Persian cat, Esme, lay curled in a padded rocker in a patch of sunshine.

Once inside the gorgeously decorated home, which always struck him as "cozy museum," he headed to the dining room, where he found Larilla seated at the head of the table, a young woman to her left. The platinum blonde looked like an extra from that movie *Working Girl* with Melanie Griffith and Harrison Ford—lots of skin, makeup and hair. They'd clearly just finished dinner, since there were serving dishes and plates on the table.

As he entered the room, the blonde let out an impressive wolf whistle and checked him out from head to toe and back up again.

Larilla jotted something down in the electronic tablet she carried everywhere.

"That's probably the kind of thing I shouldn't do anymore," the blonde said to Larilla. "It's not ladylike or whatever, right?"

"My dear," Larilla began in that slight drawl of hers, "men have been catcalling women since the dawn of time. When I was in my late forties, a man walked past me on Main Street and said, 'Hey, hot stuff.' Boy, did he end up regretting that."

The young woman's eyes widened—in a gleeful way. "Whatja do?"

Larilla took a sip of her tea. "I bored him for a good fifteen minutes in the middle of the sidewalk on why it was inappropriate to comment on my appearance—anyone's appearance, except perhaps to note that someone looked lovely today. Boring someone to death is an effective deterrent, I've noticed."

"Kinda weird for me to tell this dude he looks lovely today," the blonde said, raking her hazel eyes over him again.

"In that case, you simply ogle on the down low and keep mum," Larilla explained with a wink.

The blonde beamed, and Larilla patted her hand.

At least he understood why his godmother had asked for his help when she knew he was still bitter as hell about what happened the last time he had anything to do with an etiquette student. The platinum blonde would probably need *three* courses before she'd graduate, and by then, James would be in Europe, on a gondola in Venice. This was one student who wouldn't get to him.

Larilla turned to him. "James, I'm pleased to introduce my newest pupil, Ginger O'Leary. Ginger, my godson, James Gallagher."

"Man, your eyes are blue," Ginger said to him. "Guys get the best eyelashes too, am I right? I have to buy a new tube of mascara, like, every two weeks to keep up. Lahl!"

"Lahl?" James repeated. Was that a brand of mascara?

Ginger gaped at him as though he was nuts. "Lahl. El-oh-el. Get it?"

El-oh-el? What? Oh, he thought. *LOL*. "You mean the text acronym. Wait, so you were LOLing at your own joke? Larilla, write down that. Infraction of the worst degree."

Ginger looked worried for a second, then stared at him to see if he was kidding. Which he was. He kept his poker face, and she waved her hand in the air. "Oh God, if that's my biggest crime, I'm doing all right."

Larilla smiled. "Well, James, thank you very much. I have what I need. And, Ginger, I'll see you at 9:00 a.m. sharp for our first session."

Ginger suddenly put her hands on her stomach, and her eyes widened.

Why was she doing that? He stepped a bit closer. "Are you all right? Dinner didn't agree with you?"

"Are you kidding?" she said on a breath. "Filet mignon with roast potatoes *always* agrees with me. Like I *ever* have that."

"Then what's wrong?" he asked.

Ginger bit her lip and looked from him to Larilla and back to him. "I just felt that weird tightening sensation in my belly again. According to Dr. Google, it's normal when you're pregnant."

"Pregnant?" He stared from Ginger to Larilla.

"Ginger is in the family way," Larilla said. "She's due in December."

"If I counted right," Ginger added. "I've never been great at math."

"What did the doctor tell you?" he asked.

"What doctor? I just found out I was pregnant two days ago."

"I'll ask around for recommendations for an ob-gyn,"

Larilla said. "You'll need a checkup and prenatal vitamins."

Now it was becoming even clearer why Larilla would call him to help assess. Not only was Ginger the furthest thing from his type, not that he had one, but she was pregnant.

He was leaving town to get away from "fatherhood." The last thing he'd ever walk toward was more of that responsibility.

In fact, he felt a little better that now he could help out Larilla with this pupil. Buffalo would fly before James Gallagher fell for Ginger O'Leary.

Chapter Two

You've got to be kidding me, Ginger thought, eyeing the packet of homework that Madame Davenport had assigned the three new students as they were dismissed from the group class the next afternoon. Ginger had barely managed to graduate from high school—though she did always get As in history—because she hated homework. Homework had reminded her of school, which had reminded her of how she was treated there. Let's just say her name and nasty sayings were always written on the bathroom walls, even when half of it wasn't true. Boys had claimed she'd done all kinds of sex acts, and girls had scrawled that she had every disease there was. For the record, the only disease Ginger had ever had was the mumps in third grade.

The morning class at Madame Davenport's School

of Etiquette had been on "comportment," which Ginger had learned was a big word for *behavior*. How to act. How to be. The three new students had to stand up and share why they were taking the course, and Ginger had been honest again. Her fellow students had immediately warmed to her, which was rare in her world. One, a petite redhead named Karly, told her she should have thrown the scone at her baby daddy's nose and broken it. The other, Sandrine, a dental hygienist with great teeth, was madly in love with her boss, who had a specific type—Ginger had learned what a debutante was—and Sandrine wanted to become it.

"Comportment means that one doesn't throw baked goods at others," Ginger had said with her nose in the air.

They'd all burst out laughing, except Madame Davenport, who'd said, "One most certainly does not." But Madame had a twinkle in her eye, as always.

Crazy. Sometimes women took to Ginger and sometimes they didn't. She was glad her teacher and classmates seemed to like her because she liked them. Being liked was nice.

For homework, she had to write a one-page essay on the five no-no's of first meetings and why "one did not discuss these five topics": money, sex, politics, religion and appearance. Per Madame, one could pay a compliment but not be critical of how someone was dressed or their shape.

Madame Davenport wanted the students to look the part of the people they wanted to become, so a shopping trip was on the schedule. Madame had already taken

Karly, whose goal for the course was to get promoted to assistant editor of the *Wedlock Creek Gazette*, where she was the assistant to two editors. *You have to dress for the job you want, not the job you have*, Karly had said she'd read in *Glamour* magazine, and Madame Davenport agreed. Karly had returned from their trip to a boutique wearing a pantsuit that managed to be professional looking but not stuffy.

Now it was Ginger's turn. She wanted to look like a mother, but did she even know what mothers looked like? None of her friends back in Jackson had kids. And her hours had always meant she slept during the day and worked till the wee hours, so she wasn't exactly running into the stroller set. Madame Davenport had told her not to worry; they would look at magazines and the clothes in the boutique and try on different looks until Ginger liked what she saw.

Madame Davenport made it all sound so easy, which was why Ginger already adored her.

She made sure she was three minutes early for the 1:00 p.m. shopping trip, but when she came downstairs from her room—which was awesome, by the way—Madame was nowhere to be seen. One o'clock came and went. No Madame Davenport. And according to their private lesson this morning, being on time was *paramount*—a new word for Ginger.

Then suddenly the front door opened and there *he* was.

Serious *hawtness* in the flesh. James Gallagher. *Whoo, someone bring me a fan*. He wasn't in a suit today, probably because it was Sunday. He wore a long-sleeved button-down shirt and dark jeans, and she could barely drag her gaze off his biceps. My oh my, was he built. *Look up, Ging,* she told herself, treated to those blue eyes and sooty dark lashes, strong brows to match his straight nose. And those lips. Ooh, those lips.

One doesn't comment on appearance except to pay a compliment... "Looking fine, Gallagher," she said, practically licking her lips.

He chuckled, surprise in his expression. Come on, the man was super hot. Surely he knew. Hot men always did. Then again, he was sort of "buttoned-up," and those types tended not to know they were total Hemsworths.

"Did Larilla get in touch with you?" he asked. "She texted me that she wasn't feeling well and asked if I'd accompany you on the shopping trip. Normally one of my sisters would, but they're out of town until tonight visiting my brother at the ranch he works on."

"You're up on the 'mom' look?" she asked, raising an eyebrow.

"I used to help out Larilla a lot," he said. "I know all the 'looks'—the mom, VP, meeting the wealthy parents, be taken more seriously and every other look the students are trying to achieve."

She shrugged. "Huh. Well, in that case, hot stuff, let's go." He turned to open the door, letting her walk through first, naturally. "Am I supposed to take your arm? They do that in movies."

"Moms don't have to take arms. They have their hands full, literally and figuratively."

She tilted her head. "Say what?"

"No need to take my arm. We're not headed into the opera or a ball."

"Oh." *But what if I want to?* she almost said.

They headed down the sidewalk, passing big, beautiful houses like the etiquette school. Ginger could see Main Street up ahead. The Wedlock Creek Library was visible from where they were, and she could smell yummy bakery scents coming from the café she'd stopped in yesterday. She'd walked around for about an hour after being accepted into the school. She'd have explored more, but she got quickly tired of the gapes from strangers. *They're boobs, people!* she wanted to shout. *Big whoop!* She could blend in more easily in Jackson. Here in this small town, she stood out big-time.

James walked beside her, and Ginger could also smell *his* yummy scent, something spicy and soapy and masculine. "So Larilla says the objective is for you to look like you could go from playground to PTA meeting. Quite a difference from this look."

"Right?" she said, glancing down at her metallic silver leggings, belted tunic that didn't quite cover her tush and showed off her cleavage, and strappy sandals that wrapped around her ankles. Her toenails were each painted a different color. "Although yesterday, when I was walking around town, a little girl told me she liked my toes. So maybe I get to keep my fun toenails." She lifted her foot and gave it a wiggle. "You got kids?"

"Me?" He shook his head. "No, ma'am. I'd say anything to do with marriage and children is about ten years off in the distance when I've finally done everything I've wanted to do the past seven years."

"What have you been doing instead?"

"Raising my orphaned quintuplet half siblings," he

said. "I took them in when they were thirteen and I was twenty-one, fresh out of college."

She hadn't been expecting that. Sowing the ole wild oats was what she'd thought would come tumbling out of his mouth. Not that she thought all men were hound dogs. She just personally hadn't met one who wasn't. Then again, her circle didn't exactly include quality men. "Wait a minute. Did you say quintuplets? Huh. That couldn't have been easy. They must have been walking, talking hormones."

He laughed. "They were. I almost went bankrupt keeping them on Clearasil."

She liked the sound of his laughter. "I guess I got lucky there. I've never had a zit in my life."

"Not one?"

"Nope. I take after my mother and grandmother. Amazing skin genes. They're both gone now. Crazy that my mom will never meet my baby. Or vice versa, you know?"

He glanced at her and nodded. "Ten years from now or so, when I finally have a child, I'll feel that same way, I'm sure."

"You're really stuck on the ten years thing, aren't you? Ever heard of an oops?"

"I've heard of *oops*," he said. "I'll just make sure it doesn't happen to me."

"Condoms break, you know," she said, looking down.

He eyed her and nodded. "Stuff happens. It's the one thing I know for sure."

She lifted her chin, shaking off thoughts of Alden and condoms. "It's weird knowing my mom isn't on the earth anymore. I'd say the same for my dad, but I never knew him. What's also weird? Picking out a dad for my baby without knowing what a good dad would be like. I mean, I only know from TV shows."

"Picking out a dad?" he repeated.

"That's part of why I'm taking your godmother's etiquette course. To look the part so I can attract a good man to be a dad to my kid."

He stared at her hard for a moment.

"Why are you looking at me like I grew another boob?" she asked. "I'll be looking for a guy like you. You know—quality."

"I could be a real jerk for all you know," he said. "Step one to finding a good man? Fixing your good-guy radar. Trust no one on first glance. Make no assumptions."

"That's silly. People make assumptions about me based on how I look."

"Touché," he said. "But I'll bet a lot of those assumptions are wrong."

She tilted her head and looked at him. "They *are*. Like being hot and having big hair means I'm not going to be a great mom. Because I *will* be."

He glanced at her again, and she wondered what was going through his mind.

"Hot mama!" a man's voice called out as they turned onto Main Street.

Ginger glanced around for who catcalled her. Main Street was bustling with people, but there—she saw him, some jerk in a cowboy hat staring at her chest and wriggling his eyebrows at her. "Up yours!" she shouted back and flipped the guy the bird as she and James kept walking.

James shook his head. "Neanderthal. Who catcalls a woman—*and* when she's with a man? I could be your husband for all he knows. So rude."

Ginger laughed. Like, really laughed. Stopped-and-doubled-over-for-a-second laughed.

"What is so funny?" he muttered.

"That anyone would think I'm your wife. That we're together. Come on. I'd believe you'd date a woman who'd wear these sandals maybe, but that's about it."

He eyed the sparkly silver leggings and the practically see-through flowy tunic in black-and-white leopard print, but didn't agree or disagree. She wondered what his type was.

"Oh, we're here," he said, pointing at Best Dressed Boutique between the town florist and a hair salon. At the door, he turned to her. "Just curious. Why *do* you dress so…flashy?"

Flashy. She supposed that was a nice way of putting it. "I just always have since middle school. The shorter and tighter, the sparklier and shinier, the better. Plus you have to admit I have a slammin' bod. Why not show it off while I'm young?"

Was James Gallagher blushing? He was.

"Well then, why change your style?" he asked. "What are we doing here?"

"Because if I don't change the way I look and my big mouth and flipping the bird even when it's deserved, that jerk Alden might come take my baby. The baby he says can't even be his, even though he's the only man

I've been with in six months. And if I don't look right, like the kind of woman a guy like you would date, I'll never find a good man for my baby. I'm done with jerks and three-night stands. *D-O-N-E.*"

She didn't want to get all riled up before the big shopping trip, so to end the conversation she pulled open the door to the boutique and walked inside. And immediately got flashed a dirty look by a saleswoman. She also caught the brunette nudging the other saleswoman in the ribs. *Beyotch!*

"May I help you?" asked the brunette. Ginger studied her for a second. The saleswoman's expression barely hid her judgy disdain. Her makeup was understated, hair pulled back in a model-like ponytail and she wore a black pantsuit with black patent heels. Ginger hated that she had to admit the beyotch looked good. Elegant. And elegant was always good.

James came in behind her and smiled at the woman. "Hi, Kristen. Nice to see you."

The saleswoman looked from James to Ginger and understanding dawned. Ginger was clearly "one of those" from the etiquette school. No mistaking her for his woman in this boutique.

She wasn't sure why, but her usual take-me-as-I-am-or-talk-to-the-hand went poof. She felt…exposed, maybe. And she didn't like it.

It's a process, she reminded herself, thinking of something Larilla Davenport had said this morning. *And it's not going to be easy.*

Not much was.

* * *

James sat on the tufted velvet chaise in the changing area while Ginger was in one of the dressing rooms with two armloads of clothes the saleswomen had selected for her. He couldn't stop thinking about what Ginger had said.

Because if I don't change the way I look and my big mouth and flipping the bird even when it's deserved, that jerk Alden might come take my baby. The baby he says can't even be his, even though he's the only man I've been with in six months.

She wanted to look more presentable for her baby's sake. To *keep* her baby. Of all the students his godmother had had over the years, he didn't ever remember meeting someone in Ginger's shoes. He'd help her best he could.

The door to Ginger's dressing room opened and she stepped out. Were it not for her big blond hair and makeup, he'd never have recognized her. She wore a tailored white button-down shirt and khaki pants, neither tight nor loose, and red leather flats.

"The shoes add a delightful pop of color," the saleswoman said with a nod, looking at Ginger's reflection in the full-length three-way mirror.

Ginger was canting her head to the left and right, biting her lip, frowning as she turned this way and that as she checked herself out.

"I'd say this look would go from PTA meeting to playground to coffee with a gal pal," the other saleswoman said. "And the shoes are on sale this week only!"

Ginger stared at herself. "I don't know…"

"Oh! I know what's wrong!" the brunette said. "Come with me!"

"Uh, where?" Ginger asked, following the woman to a back corridor.

Five minutes later, the brunette returned with Ginger trailing behind her. At least, James thought it was Ginger. She had on the white shirt, khaki pants and red flats, but her face was scrubbed free of makeup, and her hair had been pulled back into a low ponytail, the long fluff of it cascading down the center of her back.

The gum was gone too.

"Who is this?" Ginger asked, eyeing her reflection.

"This is the new you!" the brunette said. "You look great. You look like every woman walking down Main Street."

Ginger stared at herself, her expression no less than glum. "I guess."

"Can't be easy changing up your whole style in ten minutes," James said.

Ginger's eyes darted to his. "How do you think I look?"

"Like every woman walking down Main Street," he said with a nod at the saleswoman. But that didn't seem right in Ginger's case. Not at all.

And weird as it was, he kind of missed her regular style. The glittery eyelids. The red lipstick. The flash and sparkle. This new Ginger was…not her. But then again, that was the point, right? She needed to look momish for a very good reason. This wasn't a makeover. It was an intervention.

"I have an idea," the saleswoman said. "This outfit is pretty standard. You can't go wrong owning these pieces. But you're not going to get used to looking completely different immediately. So why not buy it and walk around town and see for yourself how you're regarded? And how it feels to have everyone's unspoken approval. You'll be back buying out the place."

Ginger glanced at herself in the mirror again, then at the saleswoman. "I'm sorry, but there's no way I can go out in public looking like this."

James smiled. Score one for Ginger. She had moxie, that was for sure.

The saleswoman frowned. Hard. "Hello. You said you wanted to look like a mom. Now you do."

"Can't moms have a little pizzazz?" Ginger asked.

"Duh, the pop of red," the other saleswoman added, pointing at Ginger's feet.

"What do you think, James?" Ginger asked, turning to face him dircctly.

Three sets of eyes stared at him. "I think there's probably a happy medium. That's what I think."

"What does *that* mean?" Ginger asked.

"It means this may not be the right clothing boutique for you," James said. "Go change and we'll check out the other shop in town."

"Jazzy's?" the brunette saleswoman said. "Hardly mom focused. I always see your sisters going into that shop and what are they, twenty-one?"

"Well, Ginger should explore all options before deciding on a look," he pointed out.

"Yeah, she should," Ginger added, seeming very

relieved as she dashed back into the dressing room. She popped her head back out. "And I'm only twenty-four," she said before darting back in.

Twenty-four. She was so young. With so much on her plate.

He thought back to when he was twenty-one and got the news that his father and stepmother had died in the car accident. Having to tell his siblings. Moving into the big house on Sycamore Street, his life's plans changed in an instant from going for his MBA to being a father figure to five grieving thirteen-year-olds. He knew about having a lot on the plate. And his heart went out to her. James hadn't been alone in the world like she was. He had Larilla and his siblings, even if most of the time the Gallagher Five had driven him batty.

He wouldn't have survived any of it without Larilla's guidance and babysitting help. She'd been his mother's best friend and couldn't stand his father, who'd been something of a playboy until he'd fallen hard for Kerry, and the quints had come along. But when his siblings had been orphaned, Larilla had always treated them with the utmost kindness and generosity.

At least Ginger had Larilla in her corner for the next three weeks. Everyone needs a Larilla.

Ginger came out of the dressing room in her regular clothes but she looked half-dressed, and it took him a moment to realize why. The lack of makeup. With her hair pulled back, it was very clear how naturally pretty she was.

"I feel so naked," she said, popping a fresh stick of gum in her mouth.

"Don't you always?" he asked, eyeing her skimpy outfit as he escorted her to the door.

She gave him a playful shove. "I meant because I'm not wearing any makeup. I love makeup. Have I ever left my house without my red lipstick on? I honestly don't think so. Even to run out for an iced coffee."

"A red lip for daytime is a bit much," the brunette opined as James pulled open the door.

Ginger turned to her. "Honestly, miss, *you're* a bit much."

The saleswoman threw her a "how dare you" look and turned on her heel, and they left the store.

"Gonna rat me out to Madame Davenport for being rude?" Ginger asked as they headed back toward the school.

James smiled. "Is it rude to put a rude person in her place?"

"I knew I liked you," she said, beaming at him. She linked her arm around his, and he stiffened.

She dropped her own arm. "Sorry. Didn't mean to get too friendly. Not proper," she added in an upper-crust accent.

"You just startled me," he explained. "Let's just say a woman hasn't taken my arm in over a year. I'm taking a much-needed break from relationships."

"Got your heart busted?" she asked.

"Heart, pride, my trust—all of it. I'm sure you've been there."

"Actually," she said, "I've never been in love. I've *liked*, I've seriously lusted, but loved? To the point my heart broke? Nope."

He stared at her. "You're lucky."

"Lucky? I used to think something was wrong with me for not getting what all those sad songs on the radio were about. Then again, it's not like I'd really meet the man of my dreams in Busty's."

"Busty's?" he repeated.

"The exotic dance saloon I used to waitress in. That's where I met Alden, my baby's father. I liked him and was attracted to him, but I certainly wasn't in love."

"You clearly have a hell of a lot better radar for jerks than I do," he said. "I walked right into a trap." For a moment he wondered how they'd gotten on this subject, why in the world he was talking about his past with this woman. Ginger was practically a stranger. But for an almost stranger, she was so easy to talk to.

"Well, Alden wasn't looking to trap me. Just get into my pants. I should have seen that coming a mile away. Big dope," she added, conking herself on the forehead with her palm.

"I still call dibs on worse romantic past."

She laughed, and then her smile faded. "Well, I'd still like to know what it's like to feel so much for someone your heart could burst with it—in a good way or a bad way. You know?"

He glanced at her. "I guess. Once burned, twice shy is my new motto."

"I don't know, cowboy. You can't resist the siren call of attraction."

He pictured himself on a horse, wearing a Stetson. Riding off into the sunset alone. "Oh trust me, I most definitely will."

He was about to change the subject to something a lot less personal when he noticed that the guy walking down the sidewalk toward them was about to smash into a fire hydrant because his eyes were on Ginger's chest and not where he was going. "Hot, hot, hot," the idiot said before he crashed. "Ow!" he yelped.

"I get that a lot," she said. "Especially at the beach. Lots of guys trip on their leering faces."

He could only imagine how itty-bitty Ginger's bikini would be. And made out of string, most likely.

"There's Jazzy's," he said, pointing across the street, grateful for the image change in his mind of Ginger in that string bikini. "I think this shop will be more your speed but still accomplish what you want."

"Perf," she said as they headed over.

This store had a completely different vibe. The clothes were less classic, more contemporary. And the employees were a lot friendlier. Fifteen minutes later, Ginger's arms were loaded with items to try on. James waited on the love seat in the dressing area, flipping through a *People* magazine.

"Ooh, me likey!" he heard from the vicinity of her room.

He smiled. Had he ever met anyone who said *me likey*? He didn't think so.

Ginger burst out of the room, all smiles, and he put the magazine back on the side table. "How much do I love this jacket? This much!" she said, spreading her arms wide.

He had to admit, she looked amazing. The blazer was a pale pink, and there was something slightly iridescent about it. It nipped in at her waist and fitted her perfectly. Under it she wore a white shirt with a band of silky ruffles down the V-neck, no cleavage in sight. A pair of skinny jeans that molded to her "slammin' bod" but weren't too tight, and flat silver sandals finished the outfit.

"You look great!" he said. "Wow."

"Right?" she asked, beaming, turning this way and that in the three-way mirror in the dressing area. "But do I look like a mom? I kind of feel like I just look… nice."

"Nice is good to shoot for," he said. "Larilla would approve, for sure."

"Yeah?" she asked, looking at her reflection. "I never want to take off this jacket. And it doesn't even have rhinestones. I could stare at myself in this mirror all day."

He had to admit, it was nice to see the sparkle back in her eyes. "You've got a bunch more to try on. And I'll have to get to my office in about thirty minutes."

"Back in a flash," she said, zipping into the dressing room with a big smile.

Why did he have to like that smile so much?

Fifteen minutes later, she had three outfits, two dresses and three pairs of shoes. Larilla didn't have an account here, so he would need to pay. His godmother would reimburse him—the wealthy businesswoman insisted on comping a week's worth of new clothes for all of her students—but walking up to the checkout with his credit card sent a jolt of acid to his gut, reminding him of Ava and her betrayal.

Careful, he reminded himself. *You don't know Gin-*

*ger O'Leary or what she's capable of. You never know
what someone is capable of.*

"Mama got some pretty new clothes!" Ginger said,
seemingly to her belly, one hand on her stomach.

He instantly relaxed. Ginger was pregnant. *Pregnant.*
If there was anything that would keep him running for
the hills, it was that. After seven years of "parenthood"
times five, he was ready for croissants and good coffee in Paris, and the white sand and turquoise waters
of Bali. Not a baby. So he really had nothing to worry
about in terms of becoming attracted—or attached—
to Ginger O'Leary.

Phew.

Chapter Three

Ready to faint? Guess who got a B+ on her first etiquette school quiz? Ginger sat on her bed at Madame Davenport's the next day, looking over the quiz paper again. She'd only gotten two questions wrong. She'd forgotten that sex was one of the five no-no's in conversation—at Busty's she and her fellow waitresses talked about sex all the time—and what *poise* meant. Ginger had confused it with sitting straight instead of slumping, but apparently it meant *dignity of manner*.

Ginger liked that. She often didn't have dignity of manner, but she wanted it. A mother-to-be with dignity of manner would not have picked up the scone and thrown it at the jerk who told her she was low-class. Right? Ginger would have to ask what the correct response was the next time she met with Madame.

Last night, after Madame had dismissed the class, she'd run up to her room and given another fist pump at her B+, then called James, all excited about her good grade. He'd been kind of quiet on the phone, other than offering her congratulations. She tried to picture where he was, talking to her on his cell phone. Maybe lying down on his sofa in his sexy jeans and bare feet. Or maybe he'd just gotten out of the shower and was naked. Either way was fine with her.

"So what should I have done, instead of throw the scone at that jerk?" she'd asked him, flinging herself on her bed and closing her eyes, excited for his warm, deep voice to rush over her.

"Well, I guess Larilla would say to always keep your composure. To never let the other side see they got you. Which means not throwing anything. Not even saying 'screw you.' Just walking away."

"Whaaa?" she'd said. "Walk away? And let the jerks get away with being jerks? No way."

"It would be Madame Davenport's School of Etiquette approach," he said. "Reserve your dignity and don't give the jerks another thought or breath. When they go low, you go high and all that."

"I don't know," she said. "In the heat of the moment..."

"All about self-control. It's everything."

"Everything?" she repeated. "I don't know about that."

"Well, we're two very different people, aren't we," he said—a statement, not a question—and a balloon popped and wildly deflated inside her.

They sure were.

His final words swirling in her mind, Ginger now folded the quiz so that the B+ showed and slid it into the bezel of the huge round mirror at her dressing table. Then she sat down and took a good look at herself. Her hair was still damp from the shower. She twisted it into a low bun at her nape, the way the saleswoman at Jazzy's had her hair yesterday.

Huh, she thought, turning to the left and right. She'd always thought the bigger, the better, but she kind of felt like Meghan Markle with her hair like this, as though she could be sitting next to Queen Elizabeth with this do.

Now for makeup. No way was Ginger going out in public without makeup. Yesterday, when the beyotch at the snotty boutique had taken that wipe and rubbed off Ginger's makeup and had her wash her face squeaky clean, she'd felt so naked and undone. If she hadn't been hanging with James, if he'd been any other guy, she would have run back into the bathroom and put at least half her face back on. But being around James was like being around her best girls.

That was a weird thought. How could being with James be like chilling with a friend when he was such a Hemsworth? She could barely look at him without wanting to rip off his clothes and run her hands all over his chest and those muscled arms. So why would she feel okay about not having any makeup on around him?

"Who knows, right, Esme?" she asked Madame's cat, who'd come inside Ginger's room last night and slept on top of the dresser. The sleek gray-and-black cat was now grooming herself in a patch of sunlight on the windowsill. "So much info is being thrown at me it's no wonder I can't think straight."

She looked at her face, her skin, which was blemish-free and managed to be fair and rosy at the same time. *Do I really even need foundation or even powder?* she thought, putting her bottle of Covergirl back down. She leaned close and stroked a little eyeliner against her eyelids, then checked it out. Normally she'd rim the entire eye with her favorite liquid liner and then go over it with her sparkle pencil. Honestly, she thought she looked a little blah, but according to Madame Davenport, less was more. She picked up her pink tube of mascara and put some on—"enough to enhance, not overwhelm" per something she read in a homework assignment on appearance—then sat back and looked at herself.

"With my hair like this and the super light makeup, I kind of look like Mom." Ginger smiled in the mirror. Her mother had been a maid for a cleaning service, and they had to wear their hair pulled back. Ginger's mom had never worn much makeup, and now she could see how much she looked like her mother, who'd been her biggest hero. Heroine. "Whatcha think, Ez?" she asked the cat. "Do I pass as a mom?"

Her own question threw her off balance, and she leaned a hand out on the table to brace herself. The answer seemed so simple. And upsetting. *How I look won't make me a good mother. That's inside, not outside.* She'd had a good mother, so maybe it was already inside her to know what to do. But had she even ever held a baby? Nope, she didn't think so. She needed a crash course on all things baby. Maybe she'd start with that big baby shop she'd seen from the freeway. It was only about ten minutes away. She could go check it out and be back in time for her private session with Madame Davenport on the art of conversation.

Ginger got up and opened her closet, reaching for the sundress. A dress that went past her knees? She shook her head with a smile. The cotton had felt so nice against her skin in the dressing room yesterday, the soft material flowing over her curves and ending midcalf with a flounce. She slipped her feet into her new flat sandals and headed out, Esme the cat following her down the grand staircase.

There was no one around—Madame had a private session with Karly now, and Sandrine was practicing her conversation skills by making small talk with shop owners on Main Street. Ginger would have thought Sandrine had plenty of small-talk experience as a dental hygienist, but apparently she got so tongue-tied around her boss that she tended to clam up. Ginger gave Esme a scratch behind her ear, then left the Queen Anne to head to her car, the old but still-chugging little Honda that never let her down.

"Lovely day, isn't it?" a middle-aged woman asked with a smile as she passed by Ginger, a tiny white dog on a leash beside her.

Ginger glanced around to see who the woman was talking to. But they'd been the only two people there, and now the woman was halfway down the street. She glanced down at her outfit, the super cute navy sundress with little multicolored embroidered flowers on the neckline and hem, and reached up a hand to her low bun. *My new look has superpowers*, she thought with a smile.

But then a funny feeling came over her and she frowned, trying to figure out what the hell was bugging her. *The lady was nice to me, so what gives?* she wondered.

She shrugged and got in her car and drove out to the shopping center she'd seen from the freeway. Baby-Land was huge, taking up half the strip. Perfect, she thought as she parked. Everything baby was just what she needed to know about.

Inside the emporium, Ginger noticed a display of pamphlets with a sign: What Your New Baby Needs. *That's what I need*, she thought, plucking one and scanning the long list. Jeez Louise. It listed everything from car seats to baby-wipe warmers. *Well, I wouldn't want my baby to startle from a cold wipe on his or her cute little tush*, she thought. *I'm definitely getting a warmer.*

But then she started mentally calculating what just the basics would run her. A fortune. And she barely had two hundred bucks to her name. She'd had her eye on a fancy white wooden crib with ornate scrolls until she saw the price tag. Forget the matching changing table slash dresser. And why did a tiny newborn-size onesie cost so much? She was not going back to Busty's, so she'd have to figure out what kind of "reputable" job she could get.

She picked up a pair of yellow baby pajamas with tiny ducks on it, her heart melting. "Are you a boy or a girl?" she asked in the direction of her belly.

"So sweet!" said a voice, and Ginger turned to see a saleswoman smile at her before turning her attention back to folding a stack of shirts that said *Big Sister* across the front.

Ginger smiled back, but then the smile faded. Normally when she walked into a store, the salespeople tended to hover nearby and watch her because she must have looked like someone who'd shoplift. Once, a saleswoman had been staring at her as she picked up cheap bracelets, and Ginger, in her skintight minidress, had snapped, "Trust me, lady, I have nowhere to hide it if I was going to steal it. So back off."

The difference now? No one hovered. No one watched. No one assumed a damned thing about her because of how she looked, the way she was dressed. She looked "presentable" so she was considered "presentable."

Now she understood why she'd gotten that funny feeling when the woman walking the dog by her car had simply made a throwaway comment about the weather, a pleasantry. Because if Ginger had been dressed the way she had when she'd first shown up in town, that woman would have tossed her a dirty look and said nothing.

I'm the same person, she wanted to scream. *Why does showing less skin and wearing less makeup and having small hair make me worthier?*

Because that's how it is, she thought with a grimace. *That's why you're in Wedlock Creek, taking the etiquette course. It's why your hair is in a bun. Just focus on what's truly important.*

She put down the adorable onesie: $25.99. Until she got a job, she couldn't spend money on nonnecessities, and she had several months to go before she'd need to buy baby clothes.

What she definitely did need was a job—and not at a bar. *Get your life in order for this baby*, she told herself. A job, and she should start looking into places to live come June, when the course was over and she'd have to say goodbye to her fancy room at Madame Davenport's. She liked Wedlock Creek, the bustling downtown and gorgeous century-old wedding chapel she'd passed on the way out of town this afternoon. Plus James was here. And she liked James. A lot.

And considering she needed a little pick-me-up right now, she was going to find him.

Sometimes a girl just needed some James.

Just as James was leaving his office, trying to decide between chili tacos from his favorite food truck or maybe a chipotle chicken potpie from the Pie Diner, he ran smack into Ginger.

"Sorry!" he said, reaching out a hand to her shoulder. "I knocked right into you."

"I'll be honest," she said. "I called your godmother to ask where you might be, and she said you go out to lunch like clockwork at one thirty every day, so I thought I'd see if you wanted a hot lunch date."

He laughed, then realized she might take that the wrong way. "Not that that's amusing. I mean, not that it's not true. I mean, I'm not laughing because it's funny." Was his face turning the color of beets? "Forget it."

"Just admit that you think I'm funny," she said with a grin. "*And* hot."

He gave her a quick once-over. "You do look great. *Très chic.*"

"*Tray* wha?" she repeated.

"*Très chic.* Very chic. Very stylish."

"Right?" she said, giving her shoulders a little shimmy. "Do you really go out to lunch at the same time every day? At one thirty?"

"I guess," he said. "I keep to a schedule."

She eyed him as though that was a little crazy, then she peered at the plaque on the door of his office: JAMES GALLAGHER SOLUTIONS. "What do you solve?"

"I'm a consultant. Companies hire me to resolve workplace issues, human resources–related problems, that kind of thing."

"Like what?" she asked.

"Like…employees are complaining their manager is terrible and doesn't listen to their problems. If the human resources department can't fix it internally, they'll hire me to come in and work with both sides to find the solution. I have a pretty good track record."

"Huh. Howdya get so good at that kind of thing?"

"Well, when I was in college, I did a summer internship at a company and found out I was good at solving workplace issues, helping people reach compromises. I made a name for myself there, which got me a job in Human Resources at a corporation in Brewer. I moved to an even bigger company a couple years later, and since employees move around so much, I'd get calls asking if I'd consult. Three years ago, I put up my own shingle."

"Impressive," she said. "I guess that makes you a people person."

"Solving problems and being good at social stuff are two very different things. Trust me, at parties you'll find me watching the clock and slowly inching toward the door."

"I love parties," she said. "So where are we going for lunch?"

"Do you like potpies?" he asked. "The Pie Diner is my favorite lunch place in town. Or we can go for pizza, burgers, Chinese, Italian, barbecue."

"Potpies? Like the frozen kind my mom used to make in the microwave?"

"Except these are from scratch," he said.

"Count me in. Gotta love anything with the word *pie* in the name." She socked him in the ribs with a snort. "Am I right?" She snapped her fingers. "Oops. Madame Davenport told me to 'refrain from elbowing anyone in the stomach or side, even a playful punch.'"

"I can take it," he said, and for a moment he got caught in her gorgeous hazel eyes. She looked so pretty, once again because he could actually see her face, see *her*. "This way to the Pie Diner." He nodded to the left.

"Any excuse to take your arm," she said, linking hers around his.

He smiled. "You really do just say what's on your mind."

"Eh, what's the point of playing games? I like you. You clearly like me. So I'm putting it out there. You said you were taking a break from relationships. A break is meant to end at some point, so why not now? With me. I'm probably totally your type now." She frowned for a second, then gave her head a little shake, as if working something out with herself.

Crud. He didn't want to hurt her feelings. "Uh-uh. You see…"

Her face fell, then the smile, though closed lipped, returned. "Oh. Oh, no problem. I get it. You like me but not that way. I can use all the friends I can get, so no worries."

He let out a ridiculous and exaggerated sigh of relief that he immediately regretted. But nothing about this conversation *wasn't* going to be awkward. "Good."

"Good."

"Friends do this," she said, wagging a finger between their arms.

"They do," he agreed. But now he was holding his breath again. And he wasn't sure why.

How did this woman have him so off-kilter?

"Ooh, is that a taco truck?" she said, pointing across the street. "I'm dying for a taco with the works."

He grinned. "I had a chili taco on the brain earlier. Let's go. We can bring our lunch to the park," he added, upping his chin just to the left of the taco truck.

Ten minutes later, with a taco supreme for Ginger and two chili tacos for James, plus lemonades and an order of sopaipillas to share for dessert, they headed into the park. Right in front of their bench was a playground, little kids running around and climbing on the toddler structures, moms pushing babies in baby swings.

"Oh God, that's going to be me," she said as she unwrapped her taco, her gaze on the moms. "They make it look so easy."

James sipped his lemonade "You just do what's necessary. Kid falls down, you check the boo-boo. Not bleeding like crazy? Dust yourself off, kid. Little bully who won't let your kid down the slide? You get up and announce, using the royal *we*, 'We share the slide, you little turd.'"

She cracked up. "There's no way in a million years I'd ever believe you'd call a kid, even a bully, a little turd."

He grinned. "Maybe not. But sometimes I wanted to. Back when the quints were in eighth grade that first year it was just me and them? A few of them had trouble with jerks."

"I guess we all go through it at some point or another. And sometimes it never stops."

He held up his lemonade and she clinked with her lemonade.

She bit into her taco, her gaze again on the trio of mothers or caregivers keeping close watch on their toddlers on the climbing structures and slides. "I guess my days of getting serious side-eye for how I look are over. I really do look like everyone else now. And strangers smile at me now and mention the weather. It's weird because I'm the same person I was yesterday. You know what I mean?"

He glanced at her. "Appearances mean way too much. And we all know appearances can be deceiving."

"Exactly. I mean, is this me?" She waved her free hand up and down her torso.

"Maybe it is. You're just not used to it."

The frown was back. "I just don't want people to suddenly like me because I look like this. I want to be liked for who I am. But no one gave the old Ginger a chance. You wouldn't have given me the time of day or night."

She wasn't wrong.

"Anyway, eye on the prize, right?" she said, taking another bite of her taco. She grinned as she chewed. "I'll have to ask Madame if there's an etiquette-y way to eat a taco supreme. Do I have cheese and lettuce on my face?"

He looked at her, again unable to tear his gaze away from her warm, intelligent hazel eyes. One minute she was all vulnerability and the next desperate to save face, to seem unaffected. She put it out there, got hurt, then forced a smile. She probably had no idea how strong she was. "Nope. You look perfect."

"Ya think?"

He nodded. "Sorry, but yes. You look great. And no, a skintight animal-print minidress and a pound of makeup wouldn't attract me. It's a mask in itself, Ginger. It doesn't show who you are. It hides who you are."

"I don't know about that," she said, scrunching up her face. "That's my style. Or was."

"Is it a style? Or a cover-up? Maybe it was your way of hiding from the world. It's an aggressive look."

"So maybe I'm aggressive. That's not bad." She

frowned again. "Maybe it is. I'm not really sure anymore. I guess it is. God, this is confusing."

"Well, maybe think about how your aggression makes the other person feel," he said. "Attacked or on the spot or bulldozed."

"Huh. I see what you mean. I suppose when the snooty salesclerk said that thing about red lips being too much for daytime, I didn't have to insult her. She was just giving her opinion. I just didn't happen to agree. But I could have just said that—that I didn't agree. I didn't have to be a beyotch back."

By George, she got it. He could have hugged her right then.

"I owe you one," she said. "You're good to have in my corner."

He looked at her and grinned. "Technically, it's my job, remember? I deal in issues."

"Well, when I have a problem, you'll be the first person I go to, James Gallagher Solutions."

"I hope so. I'm here for you. For another month anyway."

She sat up straight and looked at him. "What happens in a month?"

"I fly away. I relax. I lie on pink beaches. I climb mountains. I sit in gondolas. I explore ruins. I don't have the schedules and needs of five siblings in my brain. I'll be gone all summer on a world tour. My biggest responsibility will be what to eat for breakfast."

She tilted her head and was quiet for a moment. "Ah, the long-awaited getaway. I can understand that. You took care of your siblings for seven years, and now that they're on their own, you can take a breather."

"Exactly."

She was quiet for a moment, then tucked the rest of her taco in the wrapper and put it in the bag.

"Full?" he asked.

She nodded and glanced at him, then at the little kids playing. A woman with a baby in a sling was watching a little boy with her same white-blond hair climb up a ladder to the short tower. "I wonder if it really is all instinct. Motherhood, I mean. Like, you get handed the baby and it's instant love, and how to be a mom comes naturally. God, I hope so."

He smiled. "I think a lot of it is instinctive. And love. And a lot of it is prep. How many books and websites and magazine articles are written about baby rearing? I read countless pieces on the needs of adolescents when my dad and stepmother died. I had no idea how to take care of them. But I had to figure it out."

She nodded. "I've been reading a little. Baby's first year kind of stuff. Did you know babies wake up every three hours?"

He mock-shivered. "There were times when one of my siblings would wake up in the middle of night, anxious about pimples or a mean girl or a date or just missing our parents. I was up a lot of very late nights with a teenager over the years. Less so now, of course."

"Sounds like it had to be hard. But kind of wonderful at the same time. All the family—even with the loss of your dad and stepmother. Five brothers and sisters.

I wish I had *one* sibling. I'd never want to be anywhere else than with my family."

He raised an eyebrow. "If you'd been raising your teenage quintuplet siblings for seven years, you'd be on the first plane to Tahiti."

"Maybe. For a few days. But then I'd want to come right back."

He shrugged, thinking she couldn't possibly know. Then again, he'd been an only for seven years until his half siblings had come along. For that long his life had been him, his mom and his dad. Then after the divorce, it was him, his mom and her best friend, Larilla. When the quints were born, he felt like his universe expanded.

"Quints run in your family?" she asked.

"More like they run in the town. Do you know about the legend of the Wedlock Creek Chapel?"

"I passed the chapel today. It's gorgeous. It looks like a wedding cake."

He nodded. "People come from all over the country to get married there. Legend says the chapel will bless you with multiples, whether through marriage, science, luck or happenstance."

"Happenstance? How is anyone blessed with multiples by happenstance?"

He darted a thumb at himself. "You're looking at it."

She tilted her head as if thinking about it. "Oh. Oh, right," she said. "Sorry."

"It's fine. And I didn't even have to get married at the chapel to get quints."

"Well, I'm scared spitless of *one* baby. You couldn't pay me to step foot in that chapel on my wedding day."

"Ditto," he said. "I'll start with one baby too."

"In ten years."

He gave a firm nod. "Right. In ten years. Minimum."

She glanced at him. "Well, thanks for lunch," she said, getting up, her lunch bag clutched in her hand. "I gotta go. Class starts soon."

He stood up, wishing she could stay just a bit longer. He could talk to her all day.

And as he watched her hurry away, he realized how much he meant that.

Chapter Four

"How much are you going to take off?" Ginger asked the next day, looking at her newly colored, very long hair in the mirror of Hair Spa, a fancy-schmancy hair salon. Her color, though hard to really see since her hair was wet, was now like the golden blond she'd been born with instead of the peroxide blond she'd had for as long as she could remember.

Her stylist put a hand on Ginger's shoulder. "I'm thinking two inches past your shoulders. So still long but not overly long."

"That sounds perfect," Amelia Gallagher said.

"Seconded!" said Merry Gallagher.

Ginger looked at the Gallagher sisters—two of James's twenty-one-year-old siblings—who'd accompanied her to the salon today for her beauty makeover.

Color, cut, makeup lesson. The sisters didn't look anything like James, and apparently took after their mother. Amelia and Merry had dark blond hair, pale brown eyes, long and elegant noses like Meryl Streep and a polish to them that must have been honed by Madame Davenport. Or maybe some women, even very young ones, were just good at this stuff.

Right now, Ginger's hair was almost to her waist. "Do what you have to do," she said and squeezed her eyes shut.

A Gallagher sister giggled. Ginger opened one eye and sent the young woman her best faux-angry look, then laughed. Then squeezed her eyes shut again. *Here goes…*

Snip. Snip-snip. Snippet-snip-snip. It was taking forever.

Ginger told the stylist to spin her around so she couldn't see herself in the mirror during the cut. As the blow-dryer started whirring, the brush pulling through her much shorter and lighter-feeling hair, the Gallagher sisters stood in front of her, murmuring their approval.

"You're going to love it, Ginger," Amelia said. "Your hair is now my length."

Ginger eyed her. Amelia's hair was well past her shoulders. Phew. Merry's was a chin-length bob with a fringe of bangs. Ginger liked Merry's hair, but she wasn't going *that* short. No way.

The blow-dryer stopped. "Are you ready to see your new look?" the stylist asked.

"I'm ready," she squeaked.

The chair was spun around. "Oh my gawd! I look

flipping awesome! I look like a newscaster!" She ran a hand down the sleek tresses, some long layers in the front. "I love it!"

After the stylist told her what products would work well in her thick hair, he left her in the hands of the makeup artist, who immediately told Ginger she had a "less is more" approach.

"That is supposed to be my motto, so I'm all in," Ginger said. Not ten minutes later, she was done. "Wow," she said, peering closer to the mirror. "I look so…natural."

"But enhanced!" Amelia said.

"You look gorge!" Merry added. "You're so pretty."

Ginger beamed. "Aww, thanks. I kind of miss my red lips though."

The makeup artist handed her a tube of lipstick. "It's called Gwen Stefani Red. For evening. And it's on me."

Ginger grinned. "Wow, thanks!"

In her new jeans, flat silver sandals and a black tank top with a square neckline stitched with tiny white stars, Ginger stood up and examined herself in the full-length mirror. "I look totally different. I didn't even know I *could* look like this." She turned to Amelia and Merry. "Like you guys."

"And your outfit and hair and makeup are still very much *you*," Amelia said.

"Madame Davenport is going to be most pleased," Merry added in an upper-crust accent with a shot of giggle.

As they left the salon, Ginger let out a giant yawn. She hadn't slept well last night, tossing and turning and thinking about James and all he'd said yesterday on that bench. About leaving. She'd been unable to stop picturing his face and the way his whole face lit up when he smiled. His amazing body, long and lean and muscular. Somehow she had to stop liking him *that* way immediately. Not only was he leaving town in a few weeks, but he had zero interest in becoming a father. And "interest in becoming a father" was numero uno on her checklist for Mr. Right.

Amelia suggested going to Coffee Zone to celebrate Ginger's new look, so off they went, settling into a back table with their iced drinks. Ginger was the only one who'd gotten a decadent treat.

"The baby likes salted caramel blondies, what can I say?" Ginger joked, taking a bite.

"I love that you do whatever you want," Merry said, pushing a swath of silky blond hair behind her ear. "If I ordered something like that, I'd feel like all eyes were on me eating it."

Ginger's eyes bugged out. "What the hell for?"

Merry shrugged. "Like I shouldn't be eating junk food, I guess."

Ginger's mouth dropped open. "Please tell me you didn't learn that from the etiquette school. Because if you did, I'm dropping out. That is *B* to the *S*!"

"It's just my own stupid thing," Merry said. "James is always telling me I care too much what people think."

"Strangers especially," Amelia added, her brown eyes thoughtful on her sister. "But I know what Merry means. People judge. Especially us, since now we work for Larilla. We're expected to be perfect."

"These whoevers sitting in here expect you to be perfect?" Ginger asked. "Or *you* expect you to be perfect?"

Merry and Ginger glanced at each other. "I guess we expect it," Merry said. "We want to make Larilla proud. She's James's godmother but has become like a treasured auntie to us."

Amelia nodded. "And with everything James sacrificed for us, we owe him, you know? He loves that we're working for the etiquette school. He sees us taking it over one day—far in the future, of course. Larilla told him she hopes we will. She has two grown sons who work on Wall Street—they've never had interest in the school."

"Hold up," Ginger said, putting down the blondie, which she'd been about to take a big bite of. "Do either of you even *want* to be working at the etiquette school?"

The sisters glanced at each other and gave half shrugs.

"Honestly, Ginger," Merry said, "we don't know what we want. But with Josie doing her thing and making James nuts, we don't really want to rock the boat, I guess."

"Josie?" Ginger repeated.

"Our sister. There's three girls and two boys. Josie quit college a few weeks ago when she had only one semester to go. She wants to be a singer. She gets gigs in bars and it drives James insane. He wants her to finish college and have that as a backup and focus on more 'sensible' career pursuits."

"Ah. So you guys work at Madame Davenport's because *A*, James can see you two taking over the business one day, and *B*, because you don't know what else you'd want to do."

"Right," Merry said. "James gave up so much for all of us. He was all set to attend the London School of Economics for his MBA, but then he had to move back to Wedlock Creek. Can you imagine being twenty-one, like we are," she added, wagging a finger between her and Amelia, "and suddenly being the sole guardian of five thirteen-year olds?"

Ginger tried to imagine James at twenty-one, all set to go abroad for graduate school, and instead dealing with five grieving, hormonal new teens. Not to mention his own grief. It couldn't have been easy.

Amelia sipped her iced mocha. "He worked all day, came home at six to make dinner and get us to do our homework, help us study, stayed up all night when we were sick, and comforted us when we missed our mom and dad so much we'd just sit and cry for hours. He didn't just take care of us—he made us feel like a family even though we didn't have parents."

Merry nodded. "He didn't date either. His life was work and us. There's no way he could have fitted in a relationship back then."

"He was dating someone seriously too," Amelia said. "His college girlfriend. She dumped him so fast after he moved back home to take care of us."

"Jeez," Ginger muttered. No wonder James was so ready to fly the coop and see the world. Not only had had he been weighed down with heavy responsibilities the past seven years, he'd been through the romantic wringer—twice, apparently.

And no wonder he couldn't even imagine starting a family before a decade from now. Ginger totally got it.

"All I know is that we owe him," Amelia said. "I wish Josie felt like us, but she's always marched to her own drum."

"Maybe that's a good thing," Ginger said. "Not doing something out of obligation. Finding a happy medium."

The Gallagher sisters eyed her, Merry twisting her lips as if taking that in, and Amelia giving a bit of a shrug. Ginger had her work cut out for her with these two.

Not that she should be getting involved in the inner workings of the Gallagher family. Their lives were their business. *That* should be everyone's motto.

Except if someone was on the wrong path, maybe you should point it out. Right? Then again, who said what path was wrong or right?

Argh. Why did life have to be so confusing?

"Ginger?" Merry said, a gleam forming in her eyes. "Are you going to share that salted caramel blondie or what?"

Ginger grinned and grabbed the plastic knife. "Now you're *tawking*."

As she cut the blondie into three, she pictured James and wondered what he was doing. Probably finalizing his plans for his big summer trip, fantasizing about the places he'd go and how he'd wake up with no one to think about but himself and what he wanted to do that day.

She wished he were sitting right here with them, making her laugh and giving her "that look," which meant she'd said something outrageous but had every right. He got her. He really did.

Stop thinking about him that way! she ordered herself. The man was outta here. And he wasn't remotely interested in her anyway. A little Ginger would come into the world. A decade too early for James Gallagher.

You'll be ten by the time he's ready for parenthood, she whispered silently to Bluebell, her pet name for her baby. *Me with a ten-year-old kid.* She shook her head. Crazy.

But it kept her head set on straight—her goal was to make herself into a mom, be a person whose kid couldn't get taken away, be a woman who would do right by that kid in every way, at every turn. And that included finding a father for her baby, a great guy who'd love Bluebell like his own. She had to remember that James Gallagher wasn't that guy. No matter how much she was starting to wish he was.

"No one quits college with one semester left!" James bellowed in the kitchen as he hit the on switch for the coffee maker. He needed a ton of caffeine stat. "No one!"

"Well, I did!" Josie bellowed back. "And stop telling me what to do. I'm an adult!"

Do not say, "Then act like it," he ordered himself, taking a breath and turning to face her. He had to stop being reactive and emotional, and talk to Josie adult to adult, convince her that the right thing to do was to go back to college in the fall. And since he was leaving in a few weeks, he couldn't spend the summer badgering her. He had to make her see reason before he left. Why, when he was so good at working with strangers to find solutions to their problems, could he not get through to his own sister?

Because Josie didn't think she had a problem. According to her, *he* was the problem.

"Statistics show that those who drop out of college don't return," he said, getting out a mug from the cabinet. "The best time is *now.*"

She crossed her arms over her chest. "Yes. Now is the best time for me to pursue my dreams."

Why was she so stubborn? Amelia and Merry weren't this stubborn. Neither were their two brothers. "So pursue your dreams over the summer, then go back in the fall and finish your final semester."

She gave a groan of frustration, throwing up her hands. "James. Listen. To. Me. I'm *done* with college. My GPA is terrible anyway. I was on academic probation."

He sighed. "I wished you would have called me for help, Josie. I would have driven out to your school. You know that."

She let out a breath. "I don't want help. I want to do what *I* want with my life."

Her shoulders slumped for a moment, and sadness crept into her brown eyes before she faced away from him and reached into the cabinet for a mug too.

Someone cleared her throat and it wasn't Josie. He poked his head out of the kitchen doorway and looked toward the source of the sound. Ginger and his two other sisters stood at the front door, Ginger giving him "that look" and his sisters acting fidgety.

All the fight went out of him. He hated arguing with Josie. He hated stressing out Amelia and Merry. He hated that he was so close to his long-awaited dream to see the world without a care and instead felt the weight of the world on his shoulders where Josie was concerned. He just wanted her on the right path before he left so that he wouldn't have to worry about her.

Josie, mug of coffee in hand, used the distraction to disappear, as did Merry and Amelia. But nothing could have distracted *him* from noticing Ginger's new, new look. Her hair was still blond, but a softer color like pale honey, and it was several inches shorter.

She walked toward him. "Do I smell coffee? I just had some decaf, but I'd love another cup if that's the growing-baby-friendly kind."

He nodded toward the kitchen and she followed him inside. "I'll make you a cup of decaf. You look great, by the way. Really, really great."

Now *she* crossed her arms over her chest. "Are you paid to say that?"

"Why would Larilla pay me to compliment you?" he asked.

"To win me over to the light side. Give me a boost about the new me."

"You can see for yourself that you look like the woman you want to turn into, Ginger."

"True. You're just so bossy with your sisters that I wonder if you even see me," she said.

"*Exqueeze* me?" he asked, Josie's favorite "how dare

you" query bursting out of him before he could stop himself. "Where did *that* come from? What do you know about my relationship with my sisters?"

"Uh, the entire town just heard you bossing Josie around, Gallagher. Demanding she listen to you and follow *your* way of thinking."

"Because I'm right. Because I make sense."

"Who—" she began, then bit her lip and glanced down.

Who died and left you king? was what she was going to say. He knew it. And she knew he knew.

"Sorry," she said. "Now I'm being bossy. And a jerk."

He let his head fall back as she stared at the ceiling. Then he stepped closer to her. "You're not a jerk. I'd rather you spoke your mind than didn't."

"But I don't agree with you."

"No kidding," he said. "But at least I know how you feel. And getting other points of view is good, especially from people you respect."

She put her hands on her curvy hips. "Would you respect me if I didn't look like a newscaster on her day off?"

He laughed. "Yes. Because you tell it like you see it. And you're smart. It's a good combo."

She seemed to take that in. "Stop making it hard for me to want to conk you on the head with a banana." She eyed the bunch in a bowl filled with fruit.

"Because I'm telling Josie what to do?"

"Yeah," she said. "And because you should listen more, demand less."

He sighed. "I listen."

"Oh? What are Merry's dreams for her life?"

"What?" he asked.

"Should I repeat the question?"

"She doesn't talk about her dreams."

"Does Amelia?"

He thought about that for a second. "Now that I think about it, no."

"Hmm. Two of your brothers are off pursuing their dreams. But Amelia and Merry are right here, safe and snug, aren't they?"

"Meaning?" he asked, joining the crossing-his-arms-over-his-chest party.

"Meaning that maybe they're toeing the line because they love you and care about you."

"Oh, come on," he said. "Merry and Amelia plan to take over the business from Larilla one day. They're her apprentices."

"Well, one day you should spend some time thinking about how that happened in the first place."

"I have no idea what you're talking about," he said, tired of the subject.

"Exactly. Which is why you should think about it."

Exasperating woman! He needed an escape plan, and luckily he had one. "Look, Ginger. I have a lot of work to do to take care of loose ends at the office and I need to get my ad for an administrative assistant in before five or I'll miss the deadline for the *Gazette*'s classifieds."

She canted her head, and he could see she was deep in thought. "You're looking for an admin? Why? You're gonna be gone all summer."

"My current assistant put in her notice because her husband got a great job out of state. I thought I could just handle things on my own, but there's a lot of paperwork and billing to keep track of, and I'd like to have someone in part-time over the summer."

"Great. I'll take the job," she said, extending her hand.

"Um, what?" He stared at her, waiting for the inevitable *Just kidding!*

Instead she said, "I need a job, James. A job that doesn't involve plunking shots of whiskey on sticky tables and getting leered at. The kind of job that's child-custody-friendly. That threat will be hanging over my head, you know? So I need to do things right."

Oh hell.

"You just said I was smart. And now I look very admin-y, don't I?" She flashed her pearly whites and ran a hand down her sleek honey-colored hair.

Actually, hiring Ginger made sense. She *was* smart and she needed a job, and he would be gone for the majority of the time she'd be working for him. He could do her a favor. And he'd never have to worry about being too attracted to her, falling for her, because by the time he got back, if he ever forgot she was pregnant, her baby bump would be a constant growing reminder. She'd be very pregnant by the end of August.

Win-win.

He suddenly pictured Ginger O'Leary six, seven months pregnant. On her own. The threat from that jerk hanging over her head. She was changing everything about herself to make that threat go away.

He had the sudden urge to pull her into a hug and hold her, tell her everything would be okay, that he had her back.

The best he could do was stick out his hand and say, "Welcome to James Gallagher Solutions."

The happiness on her face meant more to him than he wanted to think about.

Chapter Five

The next day, after a private lesson in social etiquette, where Ginger learned all kinds of stuff she'd forget in a hot minute—like who got introduced first, the person you were with or the host, and who to make appropriate small talk with at a dinner party, the person on your left or right—Ginger was sprung until three for the group session. Delia, James's current administrative assistant who was finishing out the week part-time, agreed to train Ginger.

They sat at Delia's desk at the front of the James Gallagher Solutions office. The place was minimalist chic, all pale gray and streamlined. Delia liked flowers, so there were a couple gorgeous arrangements scattered around. James's office was in the back, though he wasn't there now. He was meeting with a client who wanted a refresher. Also in the back was a conference room with a big square table, plus a small kitchen and bathroom. Every room was spotless. James would probably not like the condition of her bedroom at Madame Davenport's, with her class folders and notes all over every surface.

Delia, who Ginger immediately liked, was über-professional and matched the office in her steel-gray sheath dress, her silver-gray hair a sleek bob. The woman was giving her so much information her head was spinning. Ginger grabbed her school notebook from her tote bag and started writing down everything Delia said—invoicing systems, mail, answering the phone. Oftentimes, clients would call and bemoan they needed James to come in ASAP and handle disputes, and Ginger would need to be very calm on the phone and reassure the clients that James would get back to them right away.

Now a prospective new client had called, and Ginger could hear the woman squawking on the other end of the phone. "I'm going to kill my sister! She's destroying the business with her out-there ideas!"

"Rest assured that Mr. Gallagher will get back to you right away, Ms. Solero," Delia said ever so calmly. "Within five minutes."

"Oh, thank God. His reputation says he's immediate," Ginger heard the woman say on a sigh of relief.

"You can count on James Gallagher Solutions, Ms. Solero."

"Always?" Ginger asked when Delia hung up the office phone, grabbed her cell phone and then started texting.

"Always. Texting him the details now." Ginger watched her text away, her thumbs flying on the tiny keyboard before she put the phone back down. "He's likely returning her call as we speak."

"What if he's in a meeting? Or on a plane?"

Delia smiled. "Then I'd return the call with the exact time he'd get back to the person. Assurance is a huge part of James's appeal to clients and prospective clients."

Don't I know it, Ginger thought as Delia ran through some other good-to-know topics, such as where the delivery menus were stored and which eateries were quick at lunchtime.

After an hour and a half, Delia seemed satisfied that Ginger had it down and the woman had left. Ginger was on her own. In the thirty minutes that Delia had been gone, James had three calls, and she'd texted him the details. All prospective clients looking to set up introductory meetings.

When he returned a half hour later, looking hot and sharp in a dark blue suit, Ginger said in her most professional voice, "Good afternoon, Mr. Gallagher," then shot him a grin.

He grinned back. "Delia texted me that you're smart, a fast learner and 'she just gets it.'"

Ginger beamed. She knew she liked that Delia. "I had no idea business types in Brewer County had so many problems. Works out for you."

"Conflict is as old as time itself," he said. "Speaking of which, I'd like you to join me on an introductory meeting at the Solero Sisters Bakery. That way, you can see what goes on firsthand and meet the last new clients I'll be taking on before my trip. If anything comes up while I'm gone, you'll have already been looped in."

Wait—what? He couldn't be serious. "James, I may look the part of a professional, but I hardly know what to do or say in a business meeting. The only meetings I ever went to were weekly staff meetings in the back room of Busty's."

"Well then, you have experience at meetings."

She laughed. "Uh, somehow I think it's different."

"What did you discuss at Busty's meetings? Problems and how to solve them?"

"Yeah, but—"

He held up a hand. "No *yeah, buts* allowed. *Yeah, but* is about excuses and cynicism. *And* moves you forward."

Yeah, but—she'd always been a "yeah, but" kind of person. She thought *yeah, but* was about reality. *But* if she really stopped to think about it, she could have yeah butted herself right out of driving to Wedlock Creek and trying to get accepted into the etiquette school without money to pay the tuition. *Yeah, but I'm broke. Yeah, but I'll never really change anyway.*

She'd refused to let anything stop her, hadn't she?

So maybe James had a very good point.

"*And* I guess I'm going to this meeting," she said. "Good thing I wore my new pants." She'd been surprised she'd been drawn to them during her shopping trip at Jazzy's. Workish pants, the color of butter, and a matching sleeveless top with its own cool sheer watercolor-type scarf at the neck. This morning in group class at Madame Davenport's, Sandrine and Karly had told her she looked "very corporate" for her first day of training, and she'd eaten up the compliment.

"You look highly appropriate." He headed toward the door. "Ready?"

"I most certainly am," she said, even if butterflies were swirling.

If you could see me now, she thought, picturing the crew at Busty's, who'd just be waking up at this hour. The one person she wished *truly* could see her was her mom, but she always felt like her mom was watching anyway.

She left the office beside James, feeling like a million bucks.

The Solero Sisters Bakery was barely a five-minute walk from his office, so he and Ginger headed down Main Street, the late-May sunshine and warm breeze bringing people to sit outside at the cafés and restaurants. As they walked, he realized he'd sneaked at least a hundred peeks at Ginger. She was talking a mile a minute about how excited she was to be going to this meeting, giving him a rundown of everything Delia had taught her, and he could barely take his eyes off her.

But then a metallic-blue Fiat convertible zipped past and pulled into a spot in front of the expensive new Italian restaurant that had opened last month. And out walked Ava Guthrie and a tall, blond cowboy who looked like he was playing dress up. He was wearing Western-style clothes and a Stetson, and if James wasn't mistaken, he was sucking on a toothpick. Ava rushed around the car and wrapped her arms around him, giving him one hell of a kiss for Main Street in the middle of the day. Then she linked arms with him and they went into the Italian restaurant.

James stopped dead in his tracks as a rush of acid crawled inside his stomach and into his throat. His success had bought her that car. *Idiot!* he mentally yelled at himself. Why hadn't he seen Ava for what she was? How could he not have realized she was using him? A big sob story about a sick granny who didn't have health insurance and how Ava had almost bankrupted herself paying for her beloved nana's care, and suddenly he was giving her big checks. Anything to take the worry and sadness from her eyes. Of course, after, he'd discovered that Ava's only living grandmother was actually a very healthy sixty-five-year-old Pilates teacher at the local Y with two boyfriends.

"Something wrong?" Ginger asked, her hand on his arm.

"Yeah, something's wrong. I'm an idiot. That's what's wrong."

"Ooh, boy. Five minutes ago, you were God's gift to those with problems. Now you're an idiot?"

That actually almost made him feel better. "See that car? The Fiat?"

She craned her neck. "Spiffy."

"Yeah. It was the last thing I bought for a recent graduate of Larilla's before she let me know I was a sucker and 'Sorry, but I never said I was serious about you.'"

"Were you about her?" she asked.

"That's what makes me feel like an idiot. I was. I really fell for her."

She glanced at him, then at the car, then back at him. "What was so special about her?"

"I guess at first it was her combination of vulnerability and goals—she wanted so much to turn herself into someone her supposedly terminally ill grandmother could be proud of. I fell for it all. Her grandmother wasn't even sick. She just wanted a free ride while she was taking Larilla's course and needed a fool to bilk. And I fell for it."

He froze. Hadn't he been thinking recently that Ginger's vulnerability and goals had gotten to him? He mentally shook his head at himself. He had to be careful.

"I'm really sorry, James. That had to have hurt bad. Betrayal sucks."

He nodded. "It sure does."

She wrapped her arms around him and held on to him, and he felt himself stiffen. "Oh, stop it, James Gallagher. You need a hug."

He took a step back. "What I need is to keep myself focused on what I want—to leave town. To never let myself get wrapped up in someone's life."

"Good luck with that one. If you're human, you get wrapped up. It's just how life works."

"Well, I'm about sailing away. Not getting involved with anyone—especially a student of Larilla's." Oh hell. Had he said that last part? Yes, he had because Ginger had her hands on her hips and she was glaring at him.

"Are you talking about me? Clearly you are."

"I said *a* student. *Any* student. Come on, you get burned by someone in a particular place and of course you'll avoid that place. Would you really have trusted another leering customer at Busty's after what happened with Alden?"

The hazel glare continued. "I don't judge every person based on what one jerk does. Even leering Busty's customers. One person doesn't speak for a place."

She was right. Of course, she was right. But still.

"I trusted Ava and she turned out be a lie," he said, his voice low and kind of broken, making him realize how stupidly hurt he still was over what happened. A year ago too.

"You really did love her," she said, her voice low and reverent.

"It's not about that. I don't have any feelings for her. I just saw her plant her tongue in some cowboy's mouth and walk into Capanelli's Italiano, and I felt nothing but revulsion—at her, at my stupidity. I guess it's not hurt that I feel so much bitterness."

"Well, if you're thinking I'm a big fat con artist, I'm not."

"I don't think that, Ginger. But my radar wasn't working with Ava. So I'm not the most trusting guy. That's all I mean. And there's nothing between you and me, so this conversation doesn't even need to be happening." He'd said that a bit too sharply and regretted it, but hell, maybe it needed to be said and that way. There *was* something between them, something that felt more than friendship, more than boss-employee. She was inside him in the same way Ava had been, but Ginger was very different from Ava. Ginger was walking, talking honesty—and he knew it. She said what she meant.

He could not fall for her. Could. Not.

No matter what else, she was pregnant. In several months she'd be a mother. She'd have a tiny, needy baby. And everything in him had been kicking up its heels to get away from responsibility.

Get her out of your system, he ordered himself. *Somehow, some way.*

"The Solero Sisters Bakery is across the street," he said, pointing. "See the little bookstore? It's a few doors past that."

"You okay?" she asked. "Delia made it crystal clear that you are Mr. Dependable when it comes to your business, but maybe you should reschedule. You just saw your ex and—"

"And I'm fine," he muttered.

But he really wasn't. He felt jumbled inside, in a way he couldn't explain, and it had nothing to do with Ava Guthrie and everything to do with his new administrative assistant.

"No, we should be doing amazing cupcakes, quick-eat pastries *and* cakes," Antonia Solero said, glaring at her twin sister in the big kitchen of the Solero Sisters Bakery.

"Not if you look at the books, which you never do!" Geneva Solero shot back. "We make our money with cakes, but the cupcakes and pastries take tons of time. Talk some sense into her, please, James."

While James instead asked some basic questions of both sisters, regarding their hours and how the duties were split, Ginger looked from twin to twin. What she saw, besides two attractive identical twins in their late thirties, their long dark hair in matching sleek ponytails, silver aprons with *The Solero Sisters Bakery* in white type, was *anger*. The Soleros were pissed. If they were *her* clients, she'd start with that, then get to the baked goods. Or maybe their differences in how to handle their products had truly stirred up the anger, and she should focus on pure numbers—the books. Well, she wasn't the solutions expert, so she was dying of curiosity to know how James would approach this.

Wouldya listen to me, she thought. *If they were* my *clients?* She'd promoted herself to James's business partner. But then again, listening to their issues and coming up with solutions seemed rooted in common sense—above all else.

James asked more questions about the books and profits, and it was clear that the cakes *were* the moneymaker for the bakery.

"Small baked goods bring customers in!" Antonia insisted. "They sit at the little café tables. They have a complimentary cup of coffee or tea or lemon water with their scone or cupcake or chocolate croissant. And they can't help but notice the amazing display cakes."

"Our occasion cakes are what bring in profits," Geneva said, her voice tight. "We have incredible word of mouth. We don't need Joe Schmo walking in off the street for a cupcake that took time to bake and free beverages on the off chance he'll order a cake for his daughter's third birthday party."

"It's called customer service!" Antonia yelled. "Community building!"

Geneva threw up her hands. "Well, I'm the one who's going to be stuck doing most of the work, aren't I?"

"Oh, please. You know I'll be here."

"Meaning what?" James asked.

"Meaning guess who's pregnant," Geneva said. "I can forget about having a partner. So I say we also forget the baked goods and free stuff and focus on cakes that I can handle alone with our part-time assistants."

Ginger eyed Geneva Solero, her flashing dark brown eyes, the slight mist to them. The woman was angry and sad at the same time.

A half hour later, they had both sisters' sides, their schedules, their assistants' schedules, their business plan and their hopes for the future. James had asked to talk separately with each sister as well during the initial meeting, but neither Solero had been willing to be out of earshot of what the other might say. Talk about toughies.

Ginger, meanwhile, had taken "minutes," a new word she'd learned from Delia, writing down all the important bits in "bullet points." Delia had taught her all the major corporate terminology, from *not in my wheelhouse*—though everything seemed to be in James's area of expertise—to *let's put a pin in it*, which Ginger thought was especially ridiculous. If someone's idea struck you as dopey, instead of saying so, you could say "let's put a pin in it" to keep it up on the "idea board" and come back to it if necessary, not that you ever planned to. Lolsville on that one. She loved corpo-speak.

James was good, she had to give him that. He asked personal questions in a way that made it seem like he wasn't getting down and dirty in the sisters' private beeswax. He'd gotten out of Geneva that she lived in a one-bedroom condo in the same new development as her sister, and had been dating her boyfriend, a lawyer in town, for more than three years. Geneva was sure he was going to propose either on her birthday in July or Christmas. If not, definitely on Valentine's Day. Ginger wrote all that down. Antonia, meanwhile, got accidentally pregnant on her third date with a guy she'd now been seeing for all of seven weeks. They were madly in love and, though scared, were going for it.

"I was a little nervous how he'd react," Antonia said, her expression turning all dreamy. "But do you want to know what he said?"

Somehow Ginger had a feeling it was very different from Alden's reaction. She braced herself, since thinking about Alden's comments tended to bring her down.

Antonia smiled and touched her heart. "He said, 'Our future is happening now.' And then he picked me up and whirled me around and said he was glad that future was starting early because he knew on our first date that I was the one. How sweet is that?"

Knife into midsection. Ginger tried to keep a frown off her face. It wouldn't be professional to bring her personal life into this meeting. *Smile on, girl*, she ordered herself.

"And then he asked if he could come to my first prenatal appointment," Antonia continued. "He can't wait to see the ultrasound and hear the heartbeat. Otherwise I would have been all alone."

Was it hot in here? Ginger wondered. Her skin felt clammy and her throat was closing.

She'd be "all alone" at her prenatal appointment. All alone to hear the heartbeat.

So what! she yelled at herself. *And you won't be alone. You'll be with Bluebell. So chin up now!*

Geneva Solero glared at her sister. "Hello? Duh. *I* would have gone with you. You wouldn't have been alone. Stop being so dramatic. Drama doesn't get anything baked. And we have to get the cannoli going."

"Stop picking a fight!" Antonia snapped back. "Stress isn't healthy for the baby!"

Geneva rolled her eyes. "I can't say anything around here!" She threw up her arms—her trademark, Ginger noted—and both sisters crossed their arms over their aprons, reverting to their corners.

"I'll put together a solution plan and we can revisit this on the twenty-eighth," James said—fast. "Two days. Sound good?"

Both sisters looked relieved. "Sounds good," they both muttered.

As she and James left through the main bakery, James stopping to look around and jot down some observances, Ginger thought about how she'd stopped in the bakery her first day in town to soothe herself with a little something before she hit up the etiquette school. She'd sat right there, the far table, and had helped herself to the complimentary decaf, appreciating that it wouldn't hurt her paltry savings, and bought a blueberry muffin because it was the cheapest thing offered. One of the sisters had waited on her behind the counter and hadn't blinked an eye at her outfit or cleavage. She'd been perfectly nice, and Ginger had felt a little better about coming to Wedlock Creek. That kind of community *did* mean something. Antonia was definitely right about that. But Geneva was right about her take on things too. So what did you do when both sides were right?

As they walked back to the office, James asked, "So what you do think?"

"Well, luckily your schedule is clear," Ginger said. "And you'll be able to focus solely on the sisters as clients over the next few weeks. I'll keep you in caffeine at the office, don't worry."

"No, I mean, what's your take on the Soleros' situation?"

Ginger gaped at him. "You're asking my opinion?"

"I just did, didn't I?"

Huh. She hadn't been expecting that. "At Busty's we were told to 'leave the thinking to management.' Total a-holes. Like they *thought*? Ever?"

"Well, you're not in Busty's anymore, Dorothy. And I value your input."

Ginger beamed. And not because she got his *Wizard of Oz* reference. Sometimes James said stuff that went right over her head, but she always tucked the references away and looked them up later on the communal desktop in the parlor at Madame Davenport's.

"Well in that case… I think Geneva is reacting big-time emotionally to the fact that her sister is not only engaged but preggers. Everything is going to change. She's afraid she's going to lose her partner, her sister, her entire world. And Geneva has been dating her boyfriend for three years. Waiting, waiting, waiting. She probably said the same thing last year about how he'd propose on her birthday and Christmas. Now her sister is moving on without her, with the diamond ring that Geneva wants and a baby to boot. This is less about cakes versus cupcakes and more about what's *really* eating Geneva."

James stopped in the middle of the sidewalk and stared at her—in a good way. "I only got as far as the first line you said—that she's reacting to the pregnancy. It would have taken me a couple hours to get to everything you noted."

Huh. "It's *sooo* obvious. Did you see the way Geneva was blinking back tears? This isn't about whether to keep the cupcakes or the free coffee or to focus on cakes. I mean, it is—that's a profit and time issue—but the heart of the matter seems like big-time fear."

"I think you're absolutely right," James said. "I also think I'm getting consultancy help way too cheap. I'm upping your salary. You understood the situation immediately, and I could use your take on their case as I prepare a solution plan."

She was speechless for a moment. "That would be awesome," she said, trying to hold back how emotional she was. She could take a flying leap into James Gallagher's arms. No one, since her mother, had made her feel… What was the right word? *Smart?* Nah, she knew she was smart.

Special. That was how James made her feel. It was in everything—the way he looked at her like they were equals instead of how the mouthbreathers at Busty's would look at the waitresses as though they were hot bodies with nothing more to offer, the way he spoke to her with respect, the way he sought her opinion.

A warmth wrapped around her, the same kind of happy warmth she'd felt when she'd first discovered she was pregnant—well, before her own fear jumped in. Ginger O'Leary knew all about fear.

And since she had a busy day of two classes tomorrow, James asked her to spend the next couple of hours at the office, going over the plan for the Soleros. As they sat at the round table in his conference room, drinking the delicious Jamaican Me Crazy decaf coffee she insisted on stocking the kitchen with and hashing things out, Ginger was sure of one thing.

She'd fallen in love with her boss somewhere along the line.

At least now that he was taking her on as an employee, she'd soon be able to solve the problem of her and James herself.

There was a solution to everything, right?

Chapter Six

"You know who would have adored Ginger?" Larilla asked James, her gaze on the album of old photographs. "Your mother."

James sat beside Larilla on the fuchsia velvet sofa in the front parlor of the Queen Anne, the album on Larilla's lap. She tapped a photo of Tessa Gallagher, though in that picture, she was around ten years old and still named Tessa Mayhew. Larilla, also ten, had her arm slung around her best friend's shoulders as Tessa whispered something in her ear. From the look on Larilla's face, it was a juicy secret. "Tessa loved big personalities," Larilla said.

Yup. It was why she'd married James's father, whose personality had been a little too big. Larilla never spoke against James's dad, but he knew his godmother harbored hateful thoughts for the man who'd cheated on her BFF and left her with a young son to raise on her own. Not that he hadn't paid child support or picked up James every Sunday afternoon for a couple hours of father-son bonding, but once the quints were born, James had been pretty much forgotten by his father.

He'd always figured it was where he'd gotten good at finding solutions to problems. He'd needed to fix the problem of losing his dad to his new family, so James, at a very young age, had racked his brain for how to be included, but his calls had often gone unreturned. Then he'd come up with a brilliant way to be among the new Gallaghers. He'd done research on how to babysit five toddlers at once and offered himself up as a free "mother's helper" to his stepmom, who'd been thrilled to discover he was good at the job and she could disappear into her bedroom to read. That had cemented his place in his father's new family.

Larilla and his mother had done a lot of head shaking over the years back then—until Tessa Gallagher had been diagnosed with and died from ovarian cancer within two months when James was a freshman in college. How he'd gotten through that year he didn't know. His father had tried to "be there for him" by coming to visit him at school a few times, but then the visits quickly turned to phone calls and soon even those were rare. Four years later, when he'd gotten the call from the police that his father and stepmother had not survived their car accident on a rain-slicked road, he truly didn't think he could take the grief, that he had any room for it, that he would explode with the pain. But then he thought of the quints, his beautiful half siblings, all awkward and thirteen, their parents gone just like both of his were, and all he'd thought about was them. He'd rushed home, his heart having expanded after all.

"Yeah, she definitely would have," James agreed. "She liked straight shooters. And Ginger is certainly that."

He heard the front door open and footsteps on the stairs. His sisters. Two of them anyway. Josie had crazy hours since she'd gotten a job as a waitress at the Cowabunga Café, which had singing servers for birthdays and special events and "just because the manager was in the mood." Josie was proud of her job. The café was very popular, particularly with the tourists who flooded Wedlock Creek for weddings at the famed chapel. According to Amelia and Merry, Josie had made more in tips over the past month than she had in a year at her old waitressing job up at college. How was he going to convince her to go back to school in the fall?

Josie was another straight shooter. But as he heard the two sets of footsteps dash up the stairs, he knew his other sisters weren't as forthcoming about their feelings as Josie was. He'd been meaning to talk to them about what Ginger had said, that maybe they didn't want to work at the etiquette school, let alone take over someday, that maybe they wanted to explore other options but felt like they had to follow the life plan James had suggested for them. The thought made him seriously uneasy.

Had he unknowingly, unwittingly led them to believe he wanted them in Wedlock Creek, working for

Larilla so that they could learn the business and work their way up and eventually take over for her? Long widowed with adult sons who lived in New York City and had no interest in the school, Larilla adored the Gallagher girls, all three, and she'd love it if the school stayed "in the family," even if she was only godmother to him. He recalled that Merry and Amelia both were unsure about what they wanted to pursue for careers, so he'd suggested they work for Larilla and have a safe zone to think about what they wanted. But now that he thought about it, he'd been a little heavy-handed about how proud he was of them, how well they were doing, how Larilla adored them and thought they had great potential to become etiquette teachers.

Had he made them think that they owed him? He certainly hoped not.

Though he did like that they were safe and sound here in town. He couldn't watch over his brothers—they were both hours from Wedlock Creek—so having Amelia and Merry close and settled did give him comfort.

But he didn't want them at Larilla's because *he* wanted them there.

"And, my, has Ginger come along," Larilla trilled, pride in her expression. "I thought I'd have to work overtime with that one, but let me tell you, she's done twice the work in half the time."

Back to Ginger—good. Then again, he wasn't sure if he'd rather have her, or his sisters, on the brain. Both gave him agita right now. Ginger was something else— in the best way. Yesterday, as they'd spent a couple hours talking about the Solero sisters, the wise, thoughtful, insightful things she'd said had *him* writing down her ideas and comments. Because she'd homed in so well on the emotional angle, he'd been able to focus on the business end, and he'd put together a plan in record time. And there were moments when he'd look over at her, as she animatedly made a point about something, and he'd be so lost in thought over how pretty she was, how sparkly her eyes were, that he'd have to ask her to repeat herself.

If, if, if—and this was a moot point—if he *were* in the market for a relationship, which he was not, Ginger would be everything he'd ever wanted in a woman. In a partner. Except for the part about the pregnancy. When he'd envision himself holding a newborn at 2:00 a.m., a cold zap would blast him at various pulse points and he'd snap out of it—his overwhelming attraction to Ginger O'Leary on all levels. When it came to the most important thing to her right now—that she was going to be a mother, that she wanted to find a suitable father for her baby—he'd feel something shutter inside of him and he'd focus on it, holding it for a count of ten until his head was back on straight.

He wasn't going to be anyone's father—not for a good decade. And so he had to stop wanting Ginger and let her find the right guy for her.

"Dear," Larilla said, closing the album, "the gentleman I had lined up to take Ginger on her 'casual evening date' practicum tonight had to cancel. Would you mind taking over? I made reservations at the Cowabunga Café, and then figured you'd go to the fair. That would present a number of areas where you could assess how she's coming along. It's easy to regress in a relaxed setting."

Ugh. Josie worked at the Cowabunga Café. Just what he needed tonight. Hopefully, they wouldn't be seated in his sister's section.

But something occurred to him, something based on a comment Ginger had made the other day. "Larilla, what makes me—or any of these guys you trust to do the assessments on these dates—any judge of a woman's behavior? Who are we to decide if a woman is passing muster?" Suddenly, the very notion seemed truly sickening to him.

"My goodness, James, you're turning green," Larilla said. "Have some water." She filled a glass from the pitcher of lemon-infused water on the coffee table, and he sucked some down. "I think your question is a good one. A damned good one."

He raised an eyebrow. "Did Larilla Davenport just curse?" he asked.

She raised her chin. "I'm not a robot. And I don't want any student of mine to be. But the point of the dates is for the students to practice in the real world and see how their behavior affects others. The dates are of all types, all personalities, all backgrounds. You are not the typical 'date,' James—no one is. But for the man who Ginger wants, you *are*. So you're my choice for her for the assessment."

"Ah," he said, breathing a little easier. "It's easy to forget your students have very particular reasons for taking the course and want the feedback."

She nodded. "It's not about judging. It's about helping them see who they are in another's eyes. The students might not like that woman. Or they might not give a flying fig what their 'date' thinks of them. Both responses are valid. And it's all part of the process of my students figuring out who they want to be."

He reached over and kissed Larilla's cheek. "I don't know what I'd do without you. Sometimes I need someone stronger and wiser than me in my corner, and you're always there, Ril."

"And that's you for the quints," she said, squeezing his hand.

Lucky them, he thought with a scowl, twenty pound weights pressing down on each shoulder. "Except I might be messing everything up for them." He shook his head and let out a breath.

"Everything tends to 'out' as it should be in the end," Larilla said. "At least, that's my experience. But if there's conflict between you and your sisters, I hope you're dealing with it rather than not."

He nodded. "I thought I had everything figured out, all my ducks in a row so I could fly off to Paris without a care. Suddenly, the ducks are all over the pond."

Larilla smiled. "Then I suppose you'll have to handle whatever's going on." She eyed him, her kind blue eyes doing their own assessment—of him. "Are you up for the date tonight? If you've got too much on your mind, I can reschedule Ginger's casual night out."

Meaning she'd be with another man.

He sat up straight as he felt his collar tightening around his neck. What was with his reaction? The whole point of Ginger taking the course was to become "PTA material"—Ginger's words, not his—and be the woman who'd attract a wonderful father figure for her baby.

She was supposed to be going on the practice dates. And he wasn't really a great choice to assess her since he liked her as she was.

Wait a minute. This wasn't making sense. *He* wasn't making sense. What had happened to his orderly brain?

Ginger O'Leary and her shiny, sparkly self had happened, that was what. But he wasn't the guy for her; he wasn't ready or willing to be anyone's father.

"I'm fine," he said. "I'll do the assessment." But *could* he be impartial anyway, given that he did like her as she was?

"Of course," Larilla said, and he realized he'd phrased that last question out loud. In fact, Larilla was beaming. "I think it's lovely that you like her as she is, James. Because if you were looking to settle down and be a father, you are exactly the man she's looking for. So why not let her practice on you and be herself and grow into that self? She's changed a lot about who Ginger O'Leary is on the outside. That she doesn't have to change what's inside is the most important revelation she's going to have."

He sucked in a breath. "Right. Yes." His shoulders relaxed and he sat back. This wasn't about him. This was about Ginger's future.

Tonight he'd focus on making sure Ginger was truly all set to meet the guy she deserved, the right man for her and her child. Now that he was her boss, it was a bit easier to move into a professional zone than the friendship zone they'd been in. There was a remove now. And he was going to run with it. No matter how hard it was.

When Larilla let Ginger know that James would be taking her out for her "causal date assessment," Ginger had almost asked for a different guy. She was too comfortable with James herself. But did she really want to go out with some stranger who she wasn't remotely interested in impressing? With James, she didn't even have to impress.

But wasn't that the point of the dates in the first place? So she'd learn the ways of the "quality man" and could stop being a scone thrower and bird flipper?

Would she really ever stop? She did agree with the notion of self-control, of course. And poise and all that jazz. But sometimes, a jerk deserved the middle finger.

With any other man, *she'd* be doing the assessing. Listening closely. Watching carefully. People tended to tell you who they were in the first half hour of meeting them. Her mother had always said that, and Ginger knew it was true. But if you weren't paying attention, if you were distracted by a hot bod and gorgeous blue eyes, well then, you ended up in bed with a guy like Alden Arlington.

Ginger could use practice assessing quality men as father figures. But give up a night with James Gallagher? No way.

She wore her new little black dress, which could be casual or dressy depending on the heels and jewelry. Since tonight was all about casual, she put her hair in a low ponytail and wore her new cute wedge sandals and the little red polka-dot horseshoe earrings she'd bought at Jazzy's. Horseshoes were a sign of good luck. What she needed luck for tonight, she wasn't sure. James was a sure thing—of a fun time, of challenging conversation. But he was never going to be the man she wanted to find for Bluebell. And she had to accept it.

He picked her up her at Madame Davenport's, and she took his arm—casual be damned. She loved taking that arm. They strolled the ten minutes to the restaurant passing couples going and even a few brides and grooms who were either headed to the famed wedding chapel or coming from it. For these minutes, Ginger was James's woman and he was her man, and she also loved that. Nothing wrong with a little fantasy if she kept control of it, right?

Once they were seated in the Cowabunga Café, James sitting across from her at a cozy table for two, a small bowl of popcorn in the center in lieu of a romantic candle, Ginger couldn't help but notice how incredibly gorgeous James looked, particularly in the low lighting that cast shadows. He wore a chambray button-down shirt, sleeves rolled up to reveal sinewy forearms and khaki pants that managed to be incredibly sexy. She could stare at the sharp cut of his jawline all night, his long dark eyelashes. And the way his gaze would linger on her sent a rush of butterflies in her belly.

Am I actually a little nervous? she asked herself. She was. Which was strange, since she was so comfortable with James. And not strange, since she was pretty much in love with the guy. Pretty much? Who was she kidding? She loved him completely—even if she had to play tug of war with her emotions to keep herself in check.

"So let me guess," Ginger said, looking at the Cowabunga Café's menu. "I should order the mixed-green salad, dressing on the side—oh, and balsamic, not something good like creamy Italian—and a sparkling water with a twist of lime even though I'm dying for something ice-cold and sugary sweet."

That had been Sandrine's advice for tonight. Her fellow student's casual evening assessment date had also turned out to be her own boss, who helped out Larilla from time to time. Sandrine had been amazed at her luck—practicing on the guy herself, the very man she wanted to fall madly in love with her. Or maybe Larilla was one shrewd teacher, pairing her students with the objects of their affections. It was hard to tell with the crafty, Yoda-like Madame Davenport.

But the dentist who Sandrine thought was so great in the office turned out to be a major jerk on the date. When she'd told him she was thinking of ordering a cheeseburger with the seasoned sweet potato fries, he'd made a buzzer noise and said, *Do you want your dates to think you're going to get fat? And cheeseburgers are messy. Order something elegant so he thinks you're elegant. Like...the mixed-green salad, dressing on the side. Oh, and we should talk about another round of teeth whitening. You're pearly, but if you want to stand out...*

Ginger had seen red. Steam was coming out of her ears by the time Sandrine was done reporting on her evening and she'd barely gotten to the part about ordering dinner. The jerk! Her friend couldn't possibly be in love with this guy, could she?

"If I took a date here and she ordered a plain salad," James said, "I'd notice and not in a good way. That probably sounds just as judgmental, but we're at the Cowabunga Café, home of the foot-high loaded burger, not a tea with cucumber sandwiches."

Dammit. Of course that would be James's reaction. Why was he making it so hard to try to call a halt to her feelings?

"And sparkling water?" he said. "Yeah, I guess if you want. But I'd recommend the Wild West Whoo-Hoo."

She smiled. "What the hell is the Wild West Whoo-Hoo?"

"It's a nonalcoholic slushy cotton candy frozen concoction that comes in a sundae-type glass. My sisters live for those—even now that they're of legal drinking age."

"Bring on the sugar rush," she said. "Okay, so I'm getting the cheeseburger and fries. And the Whoo-Hoo."

"Ditto for me." He closed the menu and eyed her, then leaned close as if to say something, but just then the waitress came over to take their drink orders. "Phew," he said when she left. "Not my sister Josie. I'm pretty sure she's working tonight."

"Josie probably told the hostess never to seat you in her section," Ginger pointed out. "In fact, she may have even posted a small photo of you at the hostess station with *Do not put this dude in Josie's section* written on the back."

He frowned. "Well, I doubt she'd go *that* far."

Ginger was sure his sister would, actually. The hostess station at Busty's was full of photos with instructions on the backs. The waitresses loved going over them every night, indignant at some of the reasons. The real jerks got barred from the place, though that took some doing, but according to "senior management," the jerks had to be superjerks—jerks for Busty's, not just run-of-the-mill jerks.

Thank God she was out of that place. Coco had told Ginger the day she'd quit that she was thinking of writing an exposé of the place and industry, and that her time at Madame Davenport's had built up her confidence to think she could. Coco hoped to open a bar where there would be no exotic dancing and where female empowerment would be the name of the game.

"Anyhoo," James said.

"Anyhoo?" Ginger repeated. "Did you just say that?" She burst out laughing.

He narrowed his eyes at her. "It's called a transition to a new topic. That okay with you?"

"Absolutely," she said, trying not to laugh and enjoying the gleam in those blue eyes. He was hardly mad at her for making fun of him. "So…anyhoo what?"

James clasped his hands in front of him on the table. "Let's go over your checklist."

"My checklist?" she repeated.

"For the man you're hoping to meet. The father for your baby."

You, she thought. You, you, you.

But she couldn't say that. She wanted to; she'd been straightforward with him before, but she knew how he felt and she needed to respect that. "Well, first, he's family oriented. And has major integrity. He's a guy you can count on. Always. He means what he says and says what he means. He has his priorities straight. He's kind and thoughtful and cares about others. Doesn't judge—except for jerks who deserve it. And if he's hot and sexy, all the better. But not required."

The new Ginger was going to fall in love based on all the things she said—except that last bit. The old Ginger had been taken in by a cute face and a hot bod. No more.

"I like your list," he said, his blue gaze on her. "It's a good list."

You are the list! she wanted to scream and fling herself at him, wrap her arms around him and never let him go.

Wait. Wait. A. Minute. He *wasn't* the list. In fact, the most important thing she was looking for in a father for Bluebell was that he wanted to be a daddy. That wasn't James. So the fact that he matched every other hope and dream on the checklist? Moot. This was what she had to focus on—not that he was her dream man "if only this, if only that." But that he was the *furthest* thing from her dream man because of how he felt about fatherhood. Right now anyway. For ten more years.

Damn shame. But the truth would keep her head on straight and her focus in the right place. Which was not him.

She glanced up as a waitress approached with two huge frozen pink drinks. Not their waitress who'd given them menus and water and taken their drink orders. Josie.

"Oh flip," Josie said with a slight glare at her brother. "Jillian asked me take over her table because she just got a party of ten. I had no idea you were here." She set down the drinks, then turned her gaze on Ginger, her smile now warm and friendly.

"Miss? Miss?" a woman from a nearby table called. "We've been waiting for our check for fifteen minutes."

Josie glanced over. "Coming right over," she called to the woman. "Be right back to take your order," she said to Ginger, tossing a glare at her brother.

When Josie left, Ginger asked, "So you haven't talked to her?"

"What is there to say? We're at a stalemate. She says she's not going back to school and that it's her decision."

Ginger tilted her head. "So you're just gonna be mad at her?"

"Yes."

"I see. Very solution-driven answer to your problem with your sister."

"What am I supposed to do?" he asked. "I admit it, I'm stumped here."

"Listen to her?" Ginger suggested.

"Listen? She's not making sense. She's risking solid ground."

"I think you need to talk to her and listen. Really hear her."

He glanced away. "It's not your concern anyway."

She recoiled as if he'd slapped her across the face. "Fine. But you asked."

"Fine, but I'll take it from here," he responded. He picked up a Wild West Whoo-Hoo and held it toward her. "Let's toast to having a nice night. Not talking about my family issues. Okay?"

She did not pick up her drink. "Well, this is my casual date assessment, so you must be modeling what men like yourself want in a woman. Women who don't voice their opinions when it's contrary to yours. I'll take an F here because that's not me."

"Oh, come on, Ginger. I never said that."

"But you want me to stop talking."

"About this? Yes. It's my business, not yours. This isn't the office. It's my *family.*"

Which I'll never be a part of because you don't want any part of my package deal. I'm in love with you, you big dope, she thought, tears threatening—and Ginger wasn't a crybaby. *Why, when I find the right guy, is he the wrong guy? Why is life like that? I'm looking for a man who'd sacrifice his own life to take in his quintuplet thirteen-year-old half siblings. When that's exactly the reason he doesn't want to be a father for a decade.*

Grrr.

"Well, I guess you put me in my place, didn't you," she muttered, crossing her arms over her chest. She picked up her Wild West Whoo-Hoo and took a sip, needing something cold and overwhelming to distance her from James and their argument. *Poise. Self-control. You've got this*, she told herself. *Mmm, that is good. Slushy and sweet.*

"Besides," James said. "You've got quite enough to worry about without taking on my life too."

She thunked down the drink. "Oh, do I?" she whispered as she stood up and flung her napkin on the table.

"Ginger, I—" James began. But then nothing came out of his mouth. He looked defeated.

She shook her head in a slow tsk-tsk. "Good day!" she snapped like Willy Wonka at the end of the movie and huffed out, Josie Gallagher heading back toward their table with her order pad—and wide eyes.

Fantabulous. Ginger had lost her cool, did not act with poise and had made a young waitress nervous.

Big fat F coming her way. On the assessment and her life.

Chapter Seven

That went well.

And now James had no idea where Ginger was—but he'd bet money she wasn't coming back.

Josie came over and put her order pad in her apron. She glanced at him, then eyed the door. "Did—"

"Miss? Miss? We're ready to order," called a man at a nearby table.

Josie sighed. "Be right there, sir," she said.

She turned back to James. "You should go after her, you know that, right?"

"I know," he said, handing her a twenty for the drinks, then quickly kissing her cheek before rushing out.

He stood in front of the restaurant, looking in every direction, but didn't see Ginger. He tried calling and texting her, but she didn't respond.

He sighed and sat down on a bench in front of the Solero Sisters Bakery. He really messed things up. He had asked Ginger what she thought about the situation with Josie, and then jumped down her throat when she told him.

A dog barked in the distance, and he glanced over toward the sound coming from in front of the Wedlock Creek Chapel. He gasped and popped up. Ginger was beside the dog, bending down to pet it. Then she straightened and walked toward the chapel steps, the little white-and-tan dog following her as she sat down on the far left.

He jogged over. There were lots of people around, as usual, since the chapel with its legend brought tourists from all over. But despite all the people and the dog, Ginger looked so lonely sitting there by herself.

"Sometimes I forget that you're not made of titanium," he said, and her head whipped up. She stared at him for a moment, then lifted her chin and turned her focus to the little mutt, patting its head and running a hand down its floppy ears.

"What on earth would give you that idea about me?" she asked.

"You just seem so strong, so self-assured."

She let out a guffaw. "Self-assured? Are you freaking kidding? I'm taking your godmother's etiquette course for flipping's sake."

"For a reason," he said, sitting down beside her. The dog gave his leg a sniff. "Who's your buddy?"

She pointed at the silver tag on his collar. "His name is Belly. The other side of the tag says he belongs to the owner of the chapel." She patted his head. "Just look at his beautiful amber eyes. That is an old soul."

He was pretty cute, especially now that he was lying down between them, his furry chin on Ginger's foot.

"Once I'm settled, I'm gonna get a dog," she said. "Dogs never let you down. They just love you, you know?"

Knife to the heart. He'd let her down. Her baby's father had let her down.

"Ginger, I'm sorry for what I said at the restaurant. Josie's a sore subject, and I like it better when you agree with me. But I really do value your opinion. Obviously."

Finally, she gave him that Ginger-watt smile. "Duh. Someone has to set you straight and give you the what's what."

He took her hand without meaning to and held on to it. "You'll find that guy, the one from your checklist. He's out there."

I'm *that guy*, he thought. Dependable. Integrity. *I'm everything she's looking for.*

Except for the part about not being remotely interested in fatherhood or a major life responsibility for ten years. So he wasn't that guy. In the slightest.

Even though except for the part about the baby, *she* was everything *he* was looking for—if he were looking, which he wasn't. Someone he could really talk to. Someone who just seemed to get him. Someone who would set him straight when he needed a smack upside the head. Someone with the dependability and integrity she was looking for.

He mentally shook his head. If only, right?

He'd help Ginger in any way he could. He'd look out for her. He'd furnish a nursery for her. He'd do anything for her.

Because she felt like family. It was crazy, but she did. And he was nothing if not a family guy.

Again, except for that one little part about not wanting anything to do with fatherhood. Not for a good long time.

"So your dad and stepmother got hitched here?" she asked, standing up and reading the golden plaque on the side of the white double doors. The plaque was about the legend.

"Sure did. Apparently my dad figured he'd end up with twins. Kerry, his second wife, was an only child and wanted at least two in one. She was hoping for triplets. Man, was my father shocked when he found out he was getting five new kids at once."

"People really believe this legend?" she asked, glancing around at the throngs walking on the path, heading into the small chapel museum, which had photos of thousands of couples who'd married there and babies galore. His sisters loved walking through the museum. He avoided it like the plague.

Several brides and grooms, some decked out in full wedding regalia, some in cosplay, some in casual wear, took photos in front of the century-old chapel.

"There's something to the legend," James said, turning to look up at the beautiful white clapboard building. "My mother told me that my stepmother had gone to a fertility clinic, so perhaps science has the most to do with the huge number of multiples in Wedlock Creek.

They get married in the chapel to bless the science, if that makes sense."

"It does. I sure hope I'm only having one baby," she said, her hand on her belly. "I definitely couldn't handle two on my own, let alone three, four or five."

"I think you could handle anything life throws your way, Ginger O'Leary."

She looked up at him and planted a big one on his cheek. "That means a lot to me. Especially coming from the solutions guy."

He smiled. The dog licked Ginger's arm and then scampered off around the side of the chapel.

See the dog. Be like the dog. And know when it's time to go.

But instead of getting up, he stayed where he was. He didn't want to leave her.

"Excuse me?" asked a woman wearing a wedding gown. "Would you take our picture? Make sure you get the full chapel—and the plaque. Please and thank you!"

Ginger popped up and took the cell phone, snapping five shots, then handed it back.

"Thanks," the groom said before dipping his bride in a dramatic kiss.

"Hey, do that again," Ginger said, walking over to them with her hand outstretched. "I'll take the pic."

Another dip, another kiss, and Ginger was ready with the camera.

"Thanks! Wedlock Creek is as awesome as we heard!" the bride said before they headed around the side of the chapel.

"That was nice of you," James said.

Ginger grinned. "The chapel is all about love, so whether the legend is true or not, there's love and happiness all over this town. You can *feel* it. I'll bet that bride dreamed of getting married here since she was a tween."

"What was yours?" he asked, surprising himself—and Ginger, based on the look on her face. But strangely, he wanted to know. He wanted to know everything about this woman.

She shrugged. "I never really fantasized about the actual wedding. I'd always been focused on the guy. But convo during breaks at Busty's turned to dream weddings sometimes, and I always said I loved the idea of eloping somewhere amazing."

"Like where?" he asked.

"Somewhere magical and special. Like New Orleans."

He smiled at the thought of her in a poufy white dress, not caring if she got powdered sugar from her beignets all over it. "I'd like to go there one day."

"Me too," she said. "One of the waitresses at Busty's said the reason I wanted to elope was probably because I don't have family to invite. Man, did that put a gray cloud over my head for a few hours."

James took her hand and held it for a moment. "That comment sounded kind of passive-aggressive. Why'd you work there anyway? Why not a…regular bar or restaurant?"

She looked down at the granite step. "A friend worked there and she said the tips were great, twice what I'd make anywhere else. I was thinking about applying to college, just part-time to start, and I needed money, so I took the job. I felt like I had something of a family there. We celebrated birthdays, rallied during hard times. I guess that feeling was more important to me than the bad stuff, so I stayed. Yeah, there was always a beyotch or two, but they're everywhere. That feeling, like I had people that cared about me? It was everything."

"I can understand that," he said.

For a moment they just sat there, the shared experience of not having parents in the air between them.

"You know, when I quit Busty's and drove up here, I had three hours to feel anxious as hell. Heading into the unknown, 'family' gone. No one having my back. That gray cloud was over my head the whole drive."

"I've got your back, Ginger. I hope you know that."

"To a point, yeah," she said. "But you'll probably come back from Paris or Tombouctou with a fiancée, and she's not gonna want me hanging around. Trust me. Oh, awesome—the gray cloud is back."

"Ginger. First of all, I'm not looking to date, let alone get married. So there won't be a fiancée in my immediate future. Trust *me*. I'm done with relationships for a while. But no matter what, we're friends. I take the word *friends* seriously."

She glanced at him and nodded. There was something unsettled in her expression, and he wished he knew what the hell to do about it.

"I did take a couple classes," she said suddenly. "But I was always so tired during the day from working nights. Maybe now I can go to school at night. Thanks to my fancy new job, I can afford it." She gave him a smile, and he knew she was trying to change the subject for both their sakes. He hated to go with it, to sweep the heavy conversation under the ole rug, but he had no idea what to say about it. They were two trains on opposite tracks.

"Did you know that James Gallagher Solutions offers tuition reimbursement?" he asked. "That'll come in handy for you."

She grinned. "Delia didn't say anything about tuition reimbursement when we were talking benefits."

"Benefits at JGS are staff generated as needed. Delia already had a college degree and wasn't interested in further education, so it never came up. But she did partake in the airfare reimbursement program to visit sick relatives or tiny new relatives."

She gaped at him. "Well, I certainly have the best boss in town, that's for sure."

The dog came back over then, wagging its little cinnamon-colored tail. Ginger laughed and gave the dog a few pats and scratches.

The region of his chest felt way too heavy. He needed air—and he was outside. He really didn't know what he needed. But he had to get his head screwed back on straight. "Well, I have to put the finishing touches on the Solero proposal, so how about I walk you home?"

"'Kay," she said, standing up and linking her arm through his. The little dog scampered over to another couple, who oohed and aahed over his cuteness.

A beaming bride and groom came running out of the chapel. "Hey, catch!" the bride said and tossed the pink-and-red bouquet right at Ginger.

She caught it against her chest. "Congrats!" she called as the couple ran off toward a red convertible. "Guess I'm next," she said to James. "That's according to bridal legend. And everyone believes that one."

"Your checklist guy—Bluebell's father—is out there. He really is." The words actually managed to clear his stuffed head a bit. Yes, this was keeping his focus where it needed to be. On the right man for Ginger, which wasn't himself. But a moment later, a shot of acid burst up into his throat. Because the thought of Ginger with another man made him insane.

He hadn't even kissed this woman. So why was he feeling all…territorial?

You care about her, he reminded himself. *So of course you want her to find the perfect husband and father. That's all it is.*

"Too bad I can't find Checklist Guy before tomorrow at noon," she said.

He raised an eyebrow. "What happens then?"

"My first prenatal checkup. I'll get to hear the heartbeat and see Bluebell on the monitor."

He saw her bite her lip, something she rarely did, and in that instant he knew she was going to that appointment alone and wished she weren't.

"I'll go with you," he heard himself saying as if underwater.

She stared at him. "You? Why on earth?"

"Because I care about you, Ginger. And I want to go."

He could tell she was thinking about it. That it was both a good and bad idea, that relying on him for anything baby related wasn't in her best interest. He was leaving in a couple weeks—that was the one thing in his life set in stone.

"Well, in that case, thank you," she said. "I appreciate it."

His heart squeezed as it went out to her even more. She must *really* not want to go to that appointment alone. And he couldn't blame her.

He'd just told her he had her back, hadn't he? So of course he'd accompany her to her ob-gyn visit.

Tonight, when he'd be lying in bed unable to sleep, he had no doubt he'd replay this moment again and again. When the words tumbled out of his mouth.

If he wasn't careful, he'd be marrying Ginger next. Right in this chapel. And expecting octuplets.

So be careful, he warned himself. *Very, very careful.*

"How'd your assessment go?" Sandrine asked as Ginger came inside the Queen Anne.

Ginger wondered if James had sped from the porch, where he'd just said his goodbyes, to his car to flee from town. Anything to avoid going to her prenatal checkup. He'd offered because he was her friend, and she was glad she had him in her corner. End of story, case closed, stop thinking about it!

"It started out great," Ginger said, "then got awful, then got great again, then got confusing." She filled in Sandrine on some of the particulars. The good, the bad and the confusing.

Sandrine pushed her long hair behind her shoulders. "At least there were two *greats* in there. My own casual date assessment was awful and confusing. No *great* anywhere in there."

Ginger rubbed Sandrine's shoulder. She shivered just thinking about that superficial dentist telling her to order a plain salad for dinner. "But the good news is that you're probably over that veneered-out jerk."

"I'm three-quarters there," Sandrine said. "I've been crazy about him for so long it's hard for the feelings to just disappear, you know?"

"Oh, I know. I've been trying to quit my feelings for James for weeks now. And no matter what I know intellectually, my stupid heart wants him. And now guess who's coming with me to my prenatal checkup tomorrow?"

Sandrine gasped. "Wow. He must really care about you, Ging."

Ginger bit her lip. "He seems to. But he also cares about his sisters. And Larilla. He'd do anything for them. That's who he is. And lately it seems he'd do anything for me—except fall in love. I'm not what he wants in his heart of hearts."

"Freedom," Sandrine said.

"Right. And he deserves it."

"I guess we both have to work on falling out of love," her friend said. "There must be something about it in *Glamour* or *Cosmo*. I'll do an online search. I sure do have it easier than you," she added. "Falling out of love with a great guy? How are you going to do it?"

"I'm sure I won't be falling out of love anytime soon," Ginger said. "He's leaving, and I'll get my heart smashed and then I'll spend the summer getting over him only for him to come back and be my boss two feet away in the office." Yeah, that was not going to work. But no way was she giving up her job. She seemed to have a knack for that line of work.

"I've got it," Sandrine said with a snap of her fingers. "It's the only way."

Ginger grabbed her friend's shoulders. "Please tell me immediately."

Sandrine laughed. "You find Checklist Guy. Just like James said—he's out there. Find him and you find the real Mr. Right. The guy who checks *all* the boxes, particularly the one about wanting to be a father—and gives you *all* the feels."

Hmm, Sandrine was onto something there.

But was this mythical guy really out there?

Chapter Eight

"You've got a serious case of the jitters," James said as he escorted Ginger to her ob-gyn appointment.

She gaped at him in the middle of Main Street. How the heck did he know that? She'd been jumpy all morning, barely able to focus in her private session with Madame Davenport, who'd sent her "to rest, dear." And it was the same crazy butterflies in her tummy during the two hours she and James had spent at the office, doing one last proofreading and polishing of his proposal for the Solero Sisters Bakery. Three times he'd asked if she was feeling okay, if she had morning sickness or needed to lie down or take a break. She'd muddled through, but at half her usual Ginger speed. Which she'd been glad to discover was still fast.

It had taken her hours to realize what her deal was:

she *was* nervous about this afternoon's ob-gyn appointment. Nervous as hell. When she figured it out, she had an "oh, is that all?" moment, but then let herself sit with the nerves and butterflies until she was almost flattened by them.

What if something was wrong with her baby?

In that moment, when the truth of why she felt so scared hit her, she'd never felt so alone. Yes, James was right there, but he wasn't hers. A good friend and here he was, accompanying her to the appointment as he said he would. But he wasn't hers. She was alone. Really, really alone.

And I don't want to be. I can't do this alone. I don't want to do this alone. I want a life partner who'll love me and the baby. She had to find the mythical Checklist Guy. That was how she'd have all her dreams for Bluebell come true.

But now here was James, able to see what it had taken her so long to figure out. How could he know her so well? Checklist Daddy wouldn't know her at all. Right away anyway. Though James had seemed to truly "get her" from the beginning.

So just add: knows me so well *to the checklist— and voilà!*

She sighed. If only it were all that easy.

"Yup. Nervous." *Just say it. You're bursting with it.* "What if there's a problem?" Tears pricked her eyes, and she stopped walking and wrapped her arms around herself. "What if something is wrong?"

"Let's go on the assumption that everything is fine,"

he said, taking her hand and giving it a squeeze. "If, God forbid, something is wrong, we'll deal with it."

She saw him freeze at his own use of *we'll*. Maybe because she'd been staring hard at him when it came out of his mouth.

James Gallagher wasn't the kind of guy who'd correct himself with an *I mean,* you'll *deal with it.* And he didn't. "You've been feeling great, so that's probably a good sign." He squeezed her hand again and said, "Come on, kiddo, let's go."

Kiddo. She was only four years younger than he was. She had a feeling he was trying to distance himself from that *we'll*, homing in on her relatively young age in relation to his so that the *we'll* made sense to him. *She's like another kid sister*, he was probably trying to tell himself.

Everything will be fine, she told herself. *Repeat, repeat, repeat.* She did feel better, walking beside James, having him with her.

"Here we are," he said, pulling open the door to Dr. Maya Gomez's office.

It took fifteen minutes for Ginger to fill out all the paperwork. Just as she sat back down, a couple came out a side door, all smiles. They were both tall and tanned and blond and perfect. The woman was pretty far along, maybe seven, eight months, Ginger figured.

"It's a girl!" the woman trilled, waving ultrasound photos in the air.

Ginger smiled. "Congrats. I wonder what I'm having. I'm only about ten weeks along so a little too early anyway."

"Wow, you two are going to have one gorgeous kid," the woman said, looking between them. "With your blond hair and his blue eyes, or his dark hair and your greenish eyes."

James looked at her as though she had four heads. And as though he felt a little bit sick.

"James isn't the father," Ginger rushed to say—more for his benefit than anyone's. Hadn't the woman heard the old saying: when you assume, you make an ass out of you and me? An oldie but evergreen. Then again, Ginger and James *were* sitting together in an OB's office.

The woman's gaze went straight to Ginger's ringless left hand. "Oh. Sorry," she added with a twinge of pity before joining her husband at the receptionist's counter.

"Yeah, that's right," Ginger snapped. "I'm an unwed mother-to-be. Single. No need to be so judgy!"

"Jeez," the woman muttered as she turned around and held up her own left hand—empty too. "Calm down."

Oops. "I'm sorry," Ginger said. Now she was the one making an ass out of herself. "Overly sensitive today for some reason."

The woman smiled. "Oh, I hear you. That's my brother." She gestured toward the guy at the counter. "He's asking if there's such a thing as extrastrength prenatal vitamins now that I'm in the home stretch."

Ginger laughed. "Want to exchange contact info? We can start our own club of single moms."

"Love to!" she said. She and Ginger pressed their

numbers into their phones, and then the woman and her brother left.

And just like that, Ginger had a new friend named Erin.

"Only you can bite off someone's head and end up with a new bestie," James said on a chuckle.

Ginger smiled. "It's a skill." But she wasn't proud of it. Biting off heads, jumping to conclusions—all stuff she needed knocked out of her by Madame Davenport. She couldn't go around throwing scones—literally and figuratively. The new and improved Ginger didn't act like that.

"Miss O'Leary?" a nurse called from the side door.

The butterflies raced. Ginger couldn't even stand.

James peered at her. "Think positively, right?"

Right. No need to expect the worst or for the sky to fall. She took a breath and stood, and James put a hand at her back, like a husband. Like an expectant father.

Fifteen minutes later, Ginger was in a paper gown, and James, who'd left to give her privacy to change, had come back in. He sat on the chair in the corner, a weird pleasant look on his face.

She eyed him. He was a little freaked out too. He wouldn't admit it, but he was. Except his issue was about being here at all.

Dr. Gomez gave a rap on the door and came in, warm and friendly and immediately helping to set Ginger at ease. After answering a bunch of questions and conducting an exam, the doctor said that Ginger was ten weeks and three days pregnant. Her due date was late

December. She could have a Christmas or New Year's baby!

Finally, after squirting some gel on her belly, and gently moving around what she called a transducer, Ginger heard the unmistakable sound of her baby's heartbeat.

"Sounds good," Dr. Gomez said, her eyes on the monitor. "And all appears well and on target."

Ginger stared at the monitor, Bluebell's little form right there for her to see.

I will do my absolute best by you, she promised the baby.

After answering Ginger's thousand questions, the doctor let her to know to stop at the desk to schedule her next appointment and pick up her prescription for prenatal vitamins, then she left the exam room.

"Wow," Ginger said, blinking back tears as she stared hard at the little paper photograph of the ultrasound. Bluebell right there.

She glanced up at James, who had a fine sheen of sweat on his forehead.

Yup, he was sweating being here.

"I'll leave you to get dressed," he said and couldn't get out of the room fast enough.

I wish he could be your daddy, she thought, staring at the photo. *I don't even know if there* could *be a better man than James. Maybe I should start thinking less about finding a father for you and more about being the best mother I can be.*

Because no one could take James's place in what he meant to her.

* * *

James stood outside Dr. Gomez's office waiting for Ginger to come out. He was holding a bouquet of pink tulips. A display of them were in front of the florist two doors down, and he'd hurried over to buy them.

When she came out, she seemed surprised to see him. "I thought you ran screaming for the hills."

"Nope." He wanted to explain himself, but how could he? *Uh, I got a little emotionally overwhelmed seeing your baby on the monitor, hearing its heartbeat. Your baby became very real in those moments, and between that and my feelings for you, I panicked and fled.* No, he could not say all that. Ginger would, which was the difference between them. She said what was on her mind. It was one of her best qualities. "These are for you. To celebrate a great first prenatal exam."

She stood there staring at the flowers, not saying anything. Uh-oh. What had he done wrong? Weren't they the universal small token of good tidings?

She took the flowers and held them to her face and breathed them in. "Want to know something?"

He waited.

"No one's ever given me flowers before," she said. "Ever."

"Really?" He'd never spent much time thinking about Ginger's life before she came into his. But now he pictured her in her old look, tottering on five-inch heels around a bar called Busty's. Trying to meet her goals, trying to make her life work, trying to rise above. And never having a man in that life give her something so simple as a bouquet of flowers.

She nodded. "I guess the guys in my life weren't the flower-giving type. Thank you," she added.

"Bluebell is healthy and all is well," he said, his voice sounding clogged to his own ears. "Speaking of Bluebell, have you picked out names?"

She put her hand on her belly. "Yup. For a boy and a girl. But I'm keeping it a secret. Family superstition, according to something my mother told me once."

"Well, in my family, it's tradition to treat someone to dinner after good news. No assessment, no etiquette. Just celebrating."

Her face lit up, and he wanted to pull her into his arms and kiss her.

"That would be nice," she said in a faux British accent.

He smiled. "So let's go give the Solero Sisters presentation a final proofread, then we'll meet with them and then we'll go to dinner."

"Sounds like a plan," she said. And he knew he'd made her happy. Once again, he was struck by how well he did know her. Just a little change in her expression told him how she was feeling, what she was thinking.

Stop it, he ordered himself. *This doesn't matter. The two of you aren't meant to be. Just focus on work.*

As if that would help when Ginger was practically his business partner now.

They continued down the sidewalk to his office, just a couple blocks away, then huddled in the conference room with dark-roast coffee for him and that chocolaty decaf for Ginger, going over the PowerPoint presentation that showed all aspects of the Soleros' business.

An hour later, they headed to the bakery, where Geneva and Antonia were waiting for them.

James gave the sisters their handouts and started the presentation, which detailed not just profits and loss, but customer tracking; James had been tracking those figures for days, spreadsheets up the wazoo, and had been up till 2:00 a.m. finalizing the numbers.

"As you can see, customers who come in for small baked goods, such as scones or croissants, are pleased to be offered free coffee, tea or lemon water, and it tends to make them order *twice* in the same visit— the initial order as they arrive and an additional one as they're leaving, a box of cookies or cupcakes to go. Then within days, more than three-quarters of those customers order specialty cakes."

"Three-quarters?" Geneva repeated, her eyes wide. "Wow. That's huge. I didn't realize that."

He nodded. "A month ago, one customer who works for the town hall came in for a $2.75 muffin, probably enjoyed a cup or two of complimentary tea with cream and sugar, then in that same visit ordered a wedding cake for her daughter, a retirement cake for someone in her office and two birthday cakes for family parties. Her first visit was over two years ago, when she bought a single cupcake. Last week alone, twenty-two customers who came in for small baked goods called to order cakes ranging from $24 to $175."

"Huh," Geneva said. "I didn't realize the small baked goods had such an effect on repeat and bigger business." She narrowed her eyes at her sister. "But someone has to *make* all those cakes! And that someone is going to be me!"

"Well, that's where a more personal business plan comes into play," James said. "You're sisters. Family. And nothing is more important than your sisterhood. Not the bakery. Not the cakes. Not the scones. Your relationship."

James watched Geneva closely, the way her shoulders fell, the sadness in her face. The woman was focusing on the numbers with her head, but it was her heart that was being torn apart by her own outlook. And outlooks could change.

"You, Antonia," James continued, "are going to be a mother and your life is going to change. Maybe you'll be able to put in the same hours as you did before, maybe not. And you, Geneva, are going to be an aunt, and your life is going to change too. So coming up with a plan for how those changes will affect you both and how to keep customers satisfied, profits up and your relationship stronger than ever is key. I suggest we talk it out right now, envision scenarios and work up solutions that both of you feel good about."

Geneva's expression brightened. "Well, that sounds good to me. Key word being *both*. But, James, it's not as if you know what it's like to be pregnant and working in a small business." She gave the driest laugh ever. "Antonia says she'll feel this way or that, and you can theorize, but you can't account for reality."

James glanced at Ginger and gave her the slightest tilt of his head to indicate that the floor was hers, if she wanted it to be. He watched *her* closely now, and if she had any of those early butterflies, no one would ever know it. She looked cool as the ole cucumber, her expression full of equal parts confidence and empathy.

Ginger stood up. "James can't," she said, her attention on the sisters. "But I can. I'm ten weeks, three days along." She whipped her ultrasound photo from her purse. "And calling it as it is, is my middle name."

Yeah, it was. He'd made his share of mistakes in his life, but hiring Ginger? His best decision ever.

There was lots of congratulating and hand shaking, and then they got down to business.

And as he listened to Ginger talk about possible scenarios for the sisters, he wanted to jump up and clap with how sensible she was, how focused on common sense instead of emotion, which always managed to get the sisters back on track when one of them would throw out a *yeah, but*.

She was getting inside every bit of him. And no matter how many times he cautioned himself against getting too close to her, he was drawn to everything she was. Because Ginger was truly amazing.

Ginger had been on cloud nine ever since leaving the Solero Sisters Bakery. How had she known all that stuff that had come tumbling out of her mouth? She'd been articulate, professional and, most important, realistic. It wasn't like Ginger had more than a few days' experience of working while being pregnant, and she had no idea what it would be like when she was in her second or third trimester. But her proposals had made sense to both sisters, and Ginger had surprised the hell out of herself.

"You're solution oriented," James said. "Some people get fixated on the problem—who's right, who's wrong. That's where Geneva was. But you were able to talk to her in a way that made her feel heard and understood, and your ideas sounded truly viable to her. You were amazing."

She stopped and took his face in both her hands and kissed him. She meant it to be friendly, a thank-you, but then it turned into something else. Appreciation became desire. And after the moment of hesitation she felt from James, he kissed her back.

Yes! The man was kissing her. And not a peck either. A *real* kiss. Mmm, his lips were so warm and soft. Her knees were wet noodles as every nerve ending in her body was tingling. If this was how one kiss from this man affected her, what would he be like in bed?

She loved thinking about it. Wondering. Fantasizing.

But then the kiss was all over much too soon. He stepped back, cleared his throat and mumbled something about how inappropriate it was of him to kiss her given their new relationship as boss and employee.

"But it still happened," Ginger said, wriggling her eyebrows like Groucho Marx to lighten things up a bit.

He seemed to be measuring his words. Okay, fine, the man was the solution king, and being good at that probably had a lot to do with reining in impulsivity rather than creating new problems by speaking before thinking. But she sure wished James would let go a little.

"And it shouldn't happen again," he finally said. "I like you, Ginger. Clearly. And yes, I find you very attractive. But we both know why it would be a very bad idea to start something."

"Because you're leaving soon. And the thing about me being a package deal."

He nodded. "Exactly. Your priorities and mine are about as opposite as possible."

Jeez. What a sentence. What argument was there against that?

He had her there—dammit. It was all true, and there was no way around it.

"But we can't miss my niece's performance!" a woman's voice practically shrieked from a few feet away.

Ginger glanced over at her. The woman sat at a café table with a man, a baby stroller between them. The woman put her phone down on the table with a little thud.

"Well, we've tried every sitter and relative," the man said. "It's Friday night and it's two hours' notice, Angela."

James leaned closer to Ginger and said, "They're my neighbors."

He and Ginger walked over to the couple. "Hey," he said to them. "I couldn't help but hear your plight. Did you try my sisters? They love babysitting."

"Oh, hi, James," the woman said, trying to smile through her frown. "Yup and all three are busy."

James nodded. "Ginger, this is Angela and Dom

Maselo. They live two doors down from me. Angela, Dom, meet Ginger, my new assistant."

There were quick hellos and handshakes, and then Ginger beelined for the baby stroller and knelt in front of the sleeping beauty. "And who is this lil cutie?" she asked.

"Gia," Angela said, her voice full of her distracted disappointment. "She's six months old. Guess we have no choice but to stay home. We can't exactly take a baby to a school concert." She stood up and collected her and her husband's coffee cups.

A light bulb pinged on over Ginger's head. "If you're looking for a sitter, I'm available," she said, looking at the couple. She put her hand on her belly. "I'm almost three months along so I have babies on the brain. I'm happy to help out."

Angela's face brightened. Her husband visibly sagged with relief.

She bit her lip. "I should mention that I've never babysat before. I know that sounds impossible, but despite all the jobs I had since I was a teenager, from bagging groceries at the supermarket to working a taco truck to being a waitress, babysitting never came up. James can vouch for me as a responsible person though."

James looked from her to the now sort-of worried couple. Ginger could see they were weighing the choice—a newbie sitter who was game, an adult and the assistant of someone they knew, or missing their niece's performance.

"I can definitely vouch for Ginger," he said.

She smiled at him, the simple vote of confidence making her ridiculously proud. She hadn't even babysat, but he had faith in her to do a great job. She wanted to kiss him again.

"You've at least held a baby though, right?" Angela asked, hope blooming in her brown eyes.

"Uh, no, actually," Ginger admitted. "I'm an only, so no nieces and nephews of my own. Or friends with babies."

No one said anything for a moment. She understood their hesitation. This was their baby, and who'd want to leave a baby with someone they didn't know and who'd never even picked up an infant? They had no reason to trust her. But, man, did she want the gig. A few hours' babysitting would show her what she'd be in for soon, let her experience what it would feel like to be a mama, to cradle a baby in her arms, to protect the little one in her care.

"I'll babysit with Ginger," James said. "My experience is more starting at the teen years, but I've held plenty of babies and I'm sure, between us, we can handle anything that will happen in the three hours you're gone."

Ginger silenced the gasp that bubbled up in her throat. He clearly knew how much she wanted to do this, and he was making it happen for her.

Because he had feelings for her whether he wanted them or not. Whether he was leaving or not. Whether she was a package deal for life or not. And whether or not her priorities and his were opposites.

Or maybe he was just "good people." Doing her a favor, doing his neighbors a favor.

Except he'd kissed her back. Mix caring about her with kissing her? That equaled falling for her.

Suddenly her mind raced to the idea of playing house with James, of showing him how cozy and sweet a life with her and Bluebell could be. Maybe he'd even change his tune.

"You two are saints!" Dom said before his wife could utter a word. "Thank you."

Angela looked at her husband, then back at Ginger and James. "A million thanks!" she added.

Could this day go any better? Ginger wondered as they made arrangements to turn up at the Maselos' house at 5:00 p.m.

"That sure was nice of you," Ginger said to James as the couple headed toward their house with the stroller.

"They seemed really desperate and they're nice people. Plus, you really seemed to want to babysit, so…"

Yeah, yeah, she thought with a smile. *You know you want me.* "Well, thanks. I imagine taking care of a baby for a few hours is not how you planned to spend your Friday night."

"Babysitting is no trouble. You get to hand the baby back and leave after all, right?"

She must have looked as dejected as she felt because his expression turned instantly contrite.

"I mean, you won't, when Bluebell is born," he sputtered. "Of course. I just meant that I—"

So much for changing his tune. "It's okay, James. I've got babies on the brain, and you've got open skies and blue waters on the brain. I get it."

He nodded, relief lighting his features.

Then again, since he did like her "that way"—and
she knew he did—maybe playing house tonight *would*
start some sort of change in his mind. Two people falling for each other, spending the night taking care of a
sweet baby, making out on the sofa while half-heartedly
watching a rom-com? It was entirely possible he'd see
how nice such an evening could be—many of them in
a row. For the next eighteen years. For forever.

Wishful thinking? Perhaps. But sometimes people
thought they felt one way only to discover they wanted
something else entirely. *So let's show James Gallagher
the way a cozy night at home with his wife and baby
would be.*

Oh, so now she had them married? Ginger was so
happy she almost whooped out loud.

Chapter Nine

"Why won't she stop crying?" Ginger asked, wanting to cry herself. She tried shifting Gia so that she was more upright. But the baby cried harder, her tiny face angry and getting red.

She'd been babysitting all of twenty minutes, her "backup," James, watching a baseball game on the Maselos' huge-screen TV. She could tell that he was trying to let her handle things and not jump up to help. At first, she appreciated that, sure that she'd get the baby soothed and settled. But all the tips she'd studied online weren't working.

This was not going according to plan. James was supposed to be lounging on the sofa, enjoying the game, sipping a beer, digging into the Chinese food they'd ordered. Instead, Ginger was a disaster as a sitter, the baby's screeches were drowning out the play-by-play, and their chicken lo mein and beef in garlic sauce were getting cold fast.

"Let me take her," James said, getting up. "Eat a little something," he added, gesturing at the containers and their plates on the coffee table.

"No, I've got this. You eat, really. Watch the game. I'm fine." Tears pricked her eyes, and she hurried from the room so James wouldn't see the sheen forming. She headed through the sliding glass doors to the patio outside, and the baby stopped crying.

Miracle! Ginger wanted to shout, lifting the baby up high in the air with a grin on her face. "You little trickster, you just wanted some fresh air! Why didn't you say so? You almost had me thinking I'm gonna be bad at this motherhood thing."

The baby began fussing in Ginger's arms again. Her face began to crumple. The red tinge appeared on her impossibly big cheeks. Then the first *waah* split the quiet of the yard until Gia let out a bloodcurdling shriek followed by a steady stream of tears.

Oh God. What was wrong? She'd fed Gia about five minutes after arriving, the baby giving a very satisfying burp. So she wasn't hungry or gassy. Her diaper was dry; Ginger had changed her soon after she ate. And how she'd loved all that—settling herself in the glider with the baby in one arm, the bottle in the other, a burp cloth with cartoon giraffes on it at the ready. She'd felt so capable, so ready, her heart so bursting with pure joy.

And then the crying started and wouldn't stop. Hadn't Angela and Dom said that Gia was a very easy baby?

"Do you want to go into your crib? Maybe you're tired?" she asked.

"Waaaah!"

She headed back inside. "I think she might be tired."

"Didn't the Maselos say she'd be ready for bed at seven fifteen?"

An hour to go. So it was Ginger. Ginger was the problem.

"Ging, go eat," James said. "Let me try. Maybe she just needs a fresh body holding her. We're not her parents and she knows it."

Accepting defeat, Ginger carefully handled Gia to James. He cradled her upright against his chest, rubbing the baby's back.

And she stopped crying.

Ginger frowned—despite her ears being grateful— and stepped closer to James, who was rocking Gia as he shifted slowly from side to side. The baby was looking up at him, her brown eyes curious and happy. James made funny faces at her, and Gia laughed—a big hearty laugh that Ginger didn't even know babies were capable of making.

"Time for a story?" James asked, sitting down on the glider, the baby cradled against him. "Once upon a time, there was a really cute cat named Fluffers. And one day, Fluffers was so bored that he decided to ask the neighborhood dog, Bingo, if he wanted to play. Well, Fluffers marched right up to Bingo but Bingo started barking like crazy and—"

Ginger was so caught up in the story that it took her

a second to realize James had stopped because Gia had fallen asleep.

She dropped down on the sofa, her shoulders slumped. "So much for motherhood coming naturally. Maybe I can take a class somewhere. Someone told me the town rec center holds classes for parents of multiples, so maybe there's a basic motherhood class."

"Ginger, you don't need a class in basic motherhood. Like I said, Gia just needed a shift in person. Your instincts said she was tired, and I dismissed that because the Maselos said she wouldn't be tired for an hour. But you were right. Look at her."

Ginger eyed the sleeping tot. "I guess."

He smiled. "Hey. It's your first time dealing with a baby. Give yourself a break. An overtired six-month-old is very hard to deal with."

"Except for you, James Gallagher, the baby whisperer."

"Let's put her in her crib and then we can dig in," he said, getting up.

Ginger nodded and followed him to the gorgeous staircase, which was made of polished wood and had ornate details. When she'd first arrived at the house, she'd been blown away by it. It was a Colonial, according to James, from the early 1900s and had amazing period details. She'd never been in a house so fancy other than Madame Davenport's. James's house was pretty amazing, but the interior was comfort focused so she hadn't been intimidated by the grandeur. But here, with the modern artwork on the pale gray walls and the kind of furniture she'd never be able to afford, she felt like a kid playing grown-up.

She felt like the babysitter. Which she was.

The wall along the stairway was lined with black-and-white photos of Angela and Dom's wedding, and there were a bunch of baby Gia through the past months. *I want a wall of pictures like this*, she thought, her heart sagging so heavily she thought it might hit the steps.

James found the nursery, second door on the left, in soothing shades of pale yellow. The crib was like a white wooden sleigh with light blue sheets covered with silver stars. Along the wall was a matching dresser with a changing pad atop it. Everything Ginger wanted to buy for her baby was in this room.

You're working toward it, she reminded herself. *You have a great job. You're focused.* Soon she'd be done her session at Madame Davenport's and would have her certificate of etiquette, which was really just a fancy piece of paper that said she passed all her finals and was no longer a person who'd throw a scone or gave someone the finger or wore the kind of heavy makeup and teensy bits of clothing to hide, instead of truly revealing who she was. She was done with that Ginger.

Chin up, she stepped toward James. "I'd like to put her in the crib."

"Sure," he said, gently handing the baby over.

The eyes slid open. The face crumpled. "Waaah!" Gia screamed.

"Oh no," Ginger said, her own tears threatening again. Why was she so bad at this? She couldn't be. She was going to have her own baby.

"Hey," James whispered, both hands on her shoulders. "Give yourself a chance. You've got this."

She sucked in a breath. She shifted the baby in her arms, then rocked her a bit, swaying her gently from side to side. "Hush, little baby, don't say a word. Mama's gonna buy you a mockingbird. And if that mockingbird don't sing, Mama's gonna buy you a diamond ring. And if that diamond ring don't—" Ginger stopped singing when she glanced down at Gia's beautiful face. She couldn't believe it, but the baby's eyes had closed again, her breathing steady. She was asleep! "I did it!" she said. This time, tears poked from happiness. And relief.

She started singing very softly as she laid the baby down in the crib, then held her breath for a shriek. Not a peep. Gia quirked her upper lip and let out a little sigh, her chest rising and falling.

"Let's tiptoe out," James said, heading for the door.

She followed him, leaving the door ajar, illumination from the lamp in the corner giving the room a slight glow.

Ginger wanted to jump up and down. Instead, she went for Madame Davenport's old standby: poise. "All's well that ends well, right?"

"Oh please," James said, holding up a palm. "Slap me five right now."

Ginger beamed and high-fived him. "Okay, so maybe I got the hang of it."

"You always had the hang of it, Ginger. But parenting is second by second. Even experienced nannies can't always account for something changing up. You just have to adapt and go with it."

"Adapt and go with it," she repeated with a nod. "Solid advice."

"How about that Chinese food now?" he asked and opened up a palm for her to precede him down the stairs.

She eyed the baby monitor on the coffee table. They'd hear any little peep. And according to her research, she shouldn't rush in at the first squawk but should wait a good fifteen seconds to teach the baby to soothe herself.

Settled on the huge plush sofa, James clicked off the game and opened the containers of delicious-smelling food. Even lukewarm Chinese was great; that was how much Ginger loved chicken lo mein. James insisted on sharing his beef in garlic sauce, and within seconds, all the earlier stress was forgotten as she held up her noodle-full chopsticks for James to try a bite. He leaned forward and accepted it and all Ginger's nerve endings tingled—again.

"So which is harder—babysitting one baby or five thirteen-year-olds?" she asked, stealing a piece of succulent, sauce-drenched beef from his plate.

"Hmm, good question. Unlike babies, thirteen-year-olds are *capable* of speech—doesn't mean they actually tell you what's wrong though."

Ginger took a sip of her water. "What do you mean?"

"Take my brother Eli. When I moved home to take care of the quints, he went very quiet—weeks after the others had settled down to a grief-stricken acceptance. All moody. Disappearing to his room, not wanting to hang out with us. I kept asking what was wrong—beyond the obvious, I mean—and he'd say nothing and turn away.

Our other brother, Anders, couldn't get a word out of him either, and they'd been close before that."

"Did you ever find out what was bothering him?" she asked.

He nodded and paused for a moment, as if remembering was too much. "Turns out, he blamed himself for the car accident. Our dad and Kerry were driving to a friend's house, but Eli realized he'd left his baseball glove in their car and needed it for a game, so he'd called them, and my dad turned around. Five minutes later, they were rammed into by a drunk driver. When he finally told me—" He stopped and shook his head. "I'll never forget how he'd sobbed. 'It's my fault, I killed them, Daddy turned around because of me. They woulda been nowhere near that drunk if it wasn't for me.' Howling with tears, his body shaking. It almost broke me."

Tears welled in Ginger's eyes, and for a second she couldn't speak. That poor kid. And poor James. The sole responsibility for that kind of pain—times five. "I can understand that. I'm sure you did a very good job of comforting him."

"At first, nothing I said helped. He just kept shrieking that it was his fault and sobbing. So I finally realized what he needed was just to get out his secret, this terrible weight he'd been holding in, and to cry about it. To deal with it. So I took it all in and let him just cry in my arms. He gripped me so tightly I had marks on my back and sides for weeks."

"Oh, James." Ginger grabbed his arms, then realized

she was doing the same thing. She rubbed where she'd grabbed and then squeezed his hand. "How harrowing."

"The good news is I figured that going forward, nothing else would ever be as painful as that. That I could handle anything. Of course, I was wrong. There were times I leaned on Larilla, but other times, I couldn't betray confidences—like Eli's."

"Couldn't have been easy having everything fall on you. Five kids, all needing you." She shook her head. "I guess I thought all you had to do was feed them and get them off to school. But, man, that was the easiest part, wasn't it?"

He smiled and nodded. "Cooking, serving meals, their school schedules—all very predictable and clock focused. But yeah, dealing with mean-girl drama and fights and mono that took two of them out of school for six weeks, me caring for them around the clock to the point that I had to take a leave of absence from work. The flu, breakups, a failed class, a broken leg and wrist here and there. Thank God I had Larilla to deal with some of the trickier girl stuff. But I'll tell you, Amelia and Merry had their whoppers. Merry got caught stealing lip gloss once. Amelia and her boyfriend at the time cut school for a week of junior year. Anders swore he was quitting high school about eight times until I finally convinced him to see it through. And Eli never met a girl he didn't fall in love with, leaving a lot of angry exes sending all kinds of nasty things to the house, like dog poo in the mailbox."

"Jeez," Ginger said. "Seven years of that?"

"Well, the last couple of years have been pretty smooth sailing. Well, except now, with Josie."

"You know, you didn't mention Josie in that litany of teenage problems. Sounds like she was the golden quint."

He stared at her as though taking that in. "Huh. You know, I guess that's true. She always did her own thing, head down, but never gave me much trouble. Maybe that's why I'm so stuck on her doing the right thing now."

"The right thing? Or *your* right thing?" Ginger asked.

Instead of answering, he snatched a bite of lo mein with his chopsticks.

"Yeah, I thought so," she said with a smile.

They spent the next ten minutes eating and chatting about their favorite foods and drinks, Ginger unable to stop staring at James, half in awe of what this wonderful guy had been through with raising his siblings and half in pure admiration of his hotness. Finally, the food was gone and the containers tossed.

"Time for fortune cookies," James said, sitting back down on the couch and handing her a wrapped cookie.

"Ooh, I love fortune cookies. Well, the fortune more than the actual bland cookie." She opened hers, cracked the cookie in half and slid out the little white paper. "'A pleasant surprise is in store for you.'" She mock-scowled. "*Bor-ing.* Jeez."

He laughed. "Well, at least it's pleasant." He cracked his open. "Mine says 'Good luck is the result of good planning.'" He raised an eyebrow, then ate half the cookie. "Not sure I agree with that. Luck is luck. The whims of Fate."

"Or not," she said before taking a sip of her water. "I think it's saying you have to be in it to win it. Like, if you don't buy a lottery ticket, you're not going to win the lottery. That's planning your luck."

A smile slid over his handsome face. "I suppose so." He took her hand and gave it a squeeze but didn't let go. He was warring with himself again, she knew. Wanting to kiss her—wanting much more than that—but reminding himself so dully that she wasn't actually what he wanted. Why couldn't there be a fortune about that?

He put his hands on either side of her face and looked at her, and before his common sense could win out, she leaned close and kissed him.

"Why can't I resist you?" he breathed against her ear before kissing her back.

"Don't resist me," she said. "It's bad for your health." She inched closer on the sofa and then went for it, straddling him, her arms wrapped around his neck. Every nerve ending was on fire. One of his hands fisted her hair while the other caressed her back, and then both hands suddenly slid up her shirt, over the non-push-up but still sexy bra. Wait till he saw the matching white lace underwear—he'd really be unable to resist.

She was about to wiggle off him to do a slow striptease the way she used to, but she stayed put. First of all, they weren't exactly in a private place; they were babysitting in someone's home. Second, what if Gia woke up and needed her? She'd have to run up the stairs half-naked? That would hardly be hot—or appropriate.

And imagine if the Maselos came home early and there she was on the stairs, boobs and all.

He kissed her again, his hands everywhere, and she could easily feel how much he wanted her. For the moment he was giving in to how he felt, and she was running with it. They'd made a good team tonight. They had great Chinese. They were making out. This was exactly the night she'd hoped to have. He'd see that the life she could offer him was full of joy instead of heavy responsibility. Okay, maybe it was both. But the joy part was the key here.

"Waaah!"

Oh, pickles, she thought, using one of Madame Davenport's favorite phrases.

Maybe Gia would settle down.

"Waah! Waah-waah!"

"That's our cue," he said. "And not a moment too soon."

Rats. The "joy" hadn't won out. Yet anyway. The night wasn't over after all.

She got up as unawkwardly as possible, but it felt very "cold light of day," and there was nothing elegant about wriggling off him. He gave her a tight smile and she stood up, straightening her clothes as she dashed up the stairs, James behind her.

"The little sneak," she said as they peered into the now-quiet nursery. "She went right back to sleep."

He smiled, and they tiptoed back out and went downstairs into the living room.

"These things really are a curse," she said with a

grin, gesturing toward the baby monitor on the coffee table. "Things were just getting good."

"Or out of control," he countered, his expression way too serious. "I can't say one thing and do another, Ginger. But when I'm with you, that's exactly what happens. I say we can't start something—for very good reasons—and then my hands are under your shirt." He shook his head.

"Can I help it if quality men like this toned-down look and actually find it sexy?" she quipped, running a hand down the length of herself. Who would have thought that a not-clingy tank top and well-fitting jeans could turn James Gallagher to putty?

He walked over to the sliding glass doors to the patio, looking out. She could see his reflection in the pane, and he wasn't smiling in the slightest.

"James? What's wrong?"

He didn't respond right away. Then he turned toward her, his arms folded against his chest. "A couple weeks after I moved back into my house to take care of my siblings, I convinced Lizzie—my college girlfriend, who dumped me—to come over so we could talk. I was trying to get her to see that things between us didn't have to change just because I'd become the quints' guardian."

Ginger thought it was strange that she both hated hearing about the ex and wanted to hear about the ex. This woman who'd won James's heart—Ginger wanted to know every little detail about her. And felt pokes of jealousy. Especially because James looked so unhappy as he talked.

She was full of questions, but for once decided to keep quiet and let him talk at his own pace.

"Amelia and Merry and Josie couldn't stand Lizzie," he continued, turning around and coming over to the sofa. He sat down, and she moved over to the other side of the sofa, giving him some room, literally and figuratively. "They thought she was stuck-up and snooty and rude, and I guess she was, but I was young and stupid and thought I was in love."

In love. She could imagine what that would feel like, to have James's love, all that goodness, hotness, intensity, integrity focused on her. It felt like a dream, and one that wouldn't be coming true.

"Anyway," he said, "Amelia was calling me from the backyard, and I ignored her because I was working so hard in the living room to get Lizzie to agree to take me back. I thought Amelia was kidding around because she hated Lizzie and was just trying to get me to come out, so I kept ignoring her. Finally, Eli, who'd been upstairs, came rushing down the stairs and said he looked out the window and saw Amelia lying in a weird position, her face contorted in pain."

Oh boy. Ginger sat up straighter. "What happened?"

"Amelia had been climbing a tree in the yard, something she started doing after the car accident. She'd climb higher and higher and freak me out, but then she'd scramble down and I'd feel so relieved that I couldn't be mad at her for being such a daredevil. But that day she fell. From very high up."

"Was it bad?"

He nodded. "She broke her leg in two places and

one of her wrists. What's interesting is that she wasn't mad at me for ignoring her, but Eli lost it on me. 'Why didn't you check on her?' he screamed at me. 'All you care about is your girlfriend!'"

Ginger got up and walked over to him, sat down beside him, a hand on his back. "I'm so sorry, James. My God, you really were put through the wringer, weren't you?"

He gave something of a shrug. "The six of us have been through a lot, for sure." He shook his head. "Why did I tell you that story? I'm not even sure what made me think of it."

She glanced at the baby monitor. "Because we were getting hot and heavy, and the baby cried and needed us."

"I guess so. But there's something else all tied up in it, Ginger. It all feels so complicated."

"It's not," she whispered. "You want me, but you don't want the life I'm going to come with in about six months. You don't want a family now, James. And I get it, I really do. After everything you've dealt with, I can see the lure of a summer getaway—the beach and mountains and cities. You get to forget everything—home and work. And when you come back, all refreshed, you hardly want a wife and a baby to be responsible for."

He froze at the word *wife*. Which made her feel like horse dung. She didn't even know why she'd said it. It wasn't as if James Gallagher was thinking about her that way anyway. It was a far cry from liking someone and making out to getting married.

She let out a breath and sucked one in, accepting

how things were. Sometimes you just had to do that. No planning her own luck here, folks.

"Exactly," he said. "So let's keep things strictly professional from here on. For both our sakes."

"Like you can keep your hands off me," she joked, trying to lighten the mood. But she felt anything but lighthearted. Her chest felt tight, her eyes were scratchy, and the feeling reverberating in the region of her heart was called sadness. She was in love with James Gallagher and she couldn't have him.

"Waaah!"

They both looked to the monitor.

"Duty calls again," he said.

Exactly what he didn't want. Duty to a baby, to a family. She had to accept it. Maybe if she repeated it enough it would get though her thick head. All that hairspray she'd always used must have clogged things up in there because the truth wasn't getting through.

By the end of the night, there'd been no more kissing, no more touching. The Maselos came home and rushed up to see their baby. Ginger was so touched by how they'd flown up the stairs, unable to wait a second more than they had to see their little girl, to hold her.

And then there was James, backing away from the crib, probably dying to get out of here already.

No, this night had not gone the way she'd planned or hoped.

Chapter Ten

At almost two in the morning, James paced the living room of his family home, unable to sleep, unable to even go up to his room when Josie wasn't home. And he'd been pacing for hours now. At first, thinking about Ginger and what had happened earlier while they'd been babysitting had occupied his mind, to the point that he hadn't even realized Josie wasn't home.

Not that he made a point of checking on his sisters; they were adults after all. Of legal drinking age. But Josie's room was before his, and he'd been unable to help noticing that she wasn't in bed. She'd also ignored his texts—three of them.

So he paced.

Finally, at just after two, he heard a key in the lock and the door creaking open as if the person wanted to be extra quiet. He stood under the arched doorway into the foyer, arms crossed as usual these days, feeling the scowl pulling his face down. Josie was dressed like the old Ginger, in a tiny skirt, high-necked billowy black tank top and crazy platform heels, her pretty blue eyes ringed with black eyeliner. Artsy, he supposed.

"Little late, don't you think?" he asked, hoping the tattoo of three small musical notes on her shoulder were temporary fakes. They hadn't been there yesterday.

Josie jumped. "Jesus! You scared me half to death." She frowned. "And why are waiting up for me anyway?"

"Maybe if you answered your texts, I wouldn't have worried."

"Maybe I shut off my phone because I was performing at the café after my shift," she said. She gave him an eye roll and huffed past him, then whirled around. "Why even bother going on your world tour, James? Are you going to check in on us every day? How will you survive a day without knowing if we're safe?" Her voice, full of venom, had softened with that last word, and her face crumpled.

The family's safety was everything to all of them, Josie included. "You're driving me insane," she continued. "I'm a grown woman. Sorry if you don't like my choices. But they're mine to make."

He let out a breath and looked down, the fight whooshing out of him. He was striking out with everyone he cared about today. She was right. But *still*.

"Did Ginger walk out on you at the Cowabunga because of me?" she asked.

"No. She left the café because of *me*. She thinks I should listen to you more, demand less."

She smiled. "I knew I liked her. You should listen to her. And me."

"I just want you to be okay," he said, his voice cracking. He cleared his throat, hating when he got emotional in front of his siblings. He was supposed to be the strong one, the protector, and here he was, an open wound.

"I know," she said. "But have a little faith in how you've raised us the past seven years."

He was struck speechless. That had actually never occurred to him. And to hear her say it filled up his cup to overflowing.

"I guess I should," he said. "You know I love you like crazy, right?"

She flew into his arms and hugged him, and the weight of the world dropped off his shoulders. "I know. And ditto. But you have to accept that I'm my own person, with my own mind. I'm not always going to approach life the James Gallagher way."

"I do think you're making a mistake, Jo. Sorry. I'll accept it's yours to make though."

She let out a grunt of utter frustration and threw her hands up. "You're impossible!" she said before flying up the stairs.

He sighed. All that good will they'd just created between them gone in an instant.

He dropped onto the couch. He did have faith in how he'd raised his siblings the past seven years—a job made easy because of the foundation their parents had already built. But he also hadn't sacrificed so much so that Josie could end up a tawdry lounge singer in a too-short skirt, singing for tips.

Still, Josie was right about a couple things. One of them being that he couldn't try to run her life—and certainly not from abroad. The point of his trip was to abdicate all responsibility. So why was he heaping it on his own shoulders when it wasn't wanted or appreciated or even necessary?

He thought of Ginger, working so hard to be who she wanted, who she thought she had to be. She was great just as she was.

Why was everything so damned complicated and crazy all of a sudden?

His cell phone buzzed on the coffee table, and he snatched it up. Who could be calling at 2:17 in the morning?

Ginger.

"What's wrong?" he asked.

"Something," she said, her voice small and broken. "I'm at the Wedlock Creek Clinic. James, I'm so scared."

No, no, no. "I'm on my way. Stay on the phone with me. I'm on my way." Panic clawed at his gut. She *had* to be all right. The baby had to be all right.

"I have to go, James. I'm being called."

Click.

Oh God. *Please let everything be okay*, he sent heavenward and rushed out of the house.

When the pains had started an hour ago, Ginger kept thinking about one thing. One awful thing. That no one else on this earth cared about her baby. She was truly alone. James was her good friend—yes. Regardless of the push-pull, the kissing and the *this can't happen again*, he was true-blue. But he wasn't her baby's father and wasn't going to be.

I have to find Bluebell a good dad. Someone like James. This crazy crush—which was so much more than that—ends now.

Her resolution got her through the stabbing in her heart as the pains in her belly intensified. She'd thought about waking Madame Davenport or Sandrine or Karly, but some stubborn fixation on her new mission to find her baby's father kept her from reaching out to anyone.

Until she found herself in the emergency area of the town clinic, alone on a cot, waiting for the doctor to arrive. She'd needed her best friend, and James was her best friend. So she'd finally called him.

Not five minutes later, he came rushing through the curtain separating her "room" from the rest of the ER.

"What's going on? What did the doctor say? The baby is okay?"

Her relief at seeing him surprised even her. She was still scared, but at least he was here. "I haven't seen a doctor yet. A nurse who took my vitals said everything was fine on that end." She let out a series of fast breaths to ward off the pains.

He reached for her hand and held it. "How bad is the pain?"

"Every few seconds it lets up and then, whammo, stab city again."

A woman in a white lab coat and silver-rimmed

glasses came in and introduced herself as Dr. Berring. James hit her with a barrage of questions, but with a gentle smile she directed him to a chair and said she'd have to examine Ginger first.

Fifteen minutes later, after an ultrasound and blood tests, Dr. Berring diagnosed her with either a case of anxiety, gas or something-she-ate-itis.

James bolted up. "Are you sure? She's okay? The baby is okay?"

"Your baby appears perfectly fine and healthy and developing on schedule," the doctor said.

James paled a bit, then let out a heavy breath of relief and dropped into the chair.

He cared so much about her and the baby that he didn't even have the energy to correct the doctor.

After signing her release forms and cautioning her to rest and take it easy for the next twenty-four hours, the doctor left, and James moved over to the side of her bed. Ginger sat up, preparing to swing her legs over and get out of the cotton hospital gown.

"I'll wait just outside the curtain so you can change, then I'll drive you home."

"No need," she said. "For the ride, I mean. I have my car."

His eyes practically popped. "You drove here yourself? Doubled over in pain? In the middle of the night?"

"I managed. I'll have to, right? I'm on my own, James."

"Yeah, but you have people who care about you. Obviously," he added, stabbing his thumb backward at himself. "Larilla would have driven you. Or one of your classmates."

"I know. But I also know that I'm alone. It's me and the baby. There's no one else, no one who's going to run to rescue me every time something goes wrong. I need to stand on my own two feet."

"Ginger, what do you think friends are for?"

She turned away as tears stung the backs of her eyes. "Are we friends, James? Is that what we are?"

What was she even saying? she wondered. A few minutes ago, she'd thought of him as her best friend. He was. But he also wasn't. Because she was in love with him. And that threw everything off between them.

He stared at her—hard—his expression full of discomfort.

"I knew I loved this baby, wanted this baby," she said, her hand on her belly. "But until those pains started and I thought something might be wrong, that I might lose Bluebell—whoa. I had *no* idea how much I love and want this baby. No flipping idea, James. And now I also know that I really have to commit to finding a good father for him or her. That's the whole point, right? Everything I'm doing is for the baby."

He was quiet but seemed consumed by thought. He gave something of a nod and then said, "I'll let you get changed." He rushed through the divide in the curtain as quickly as he'd come in, this time not able to get away fast enough.

"Where's Ginger?" a voice called. A female voice. Was that his sister Josie?

"She's in there," she heard James say. "She and the baby are fine."

"Oh, thank God," Josie said. "Ginger? Can I come in?"

Surprised, Ginger sat back down on the bed. "Sure."

"Uh, I'm gonna go grab a cup of coffee," James said from the other side of the curtain. "Can I get either of you anything?"

"No, but thanks," they both said.

Josie, looking a lot like Ginger used to look, crazy platform high-heeled shoes in her hand, came in and gave Ginger a quick hug. "I'd just gotten home and gone upstairs to get ready for bed when I heard James on the phone. He left so fast I couldn't tell him to wait for me, so I followed him. I'm so relieved to hear you're okay."

Ginger reached for Josie's hand. "Thank you. It means a lot that you came." Ginger was really surprised. She would have expected Josie to just go to sleep and wait for her brother to come home with news. But instead, she'd been concerned and raced to the clinic in the middle of the night.

"Not that I'm surprised James left so fast. He was seriously speeding. He's lucky he didn't get pulled over."

"Or in an accident," Ginger said. "He sure was worried about me. The guy really cares about people, doesn't he?" she added, shaking her head with a smile. "He's a good guy to have in your corner."

"Sometimes there's too *much* James in your corner," Josie mumbled, but Ginger heard her loud and clear. "My corner."

"He adores you, Josie. I do wish he'd truly listen to your point of view though."

Josie sighed. "Well, I'm going to push back. I hate having to do it though. I mean, James really sacrificed for me—and my siblings. He gave up so much it's crazy. He'd lost his girlfriend at the time—who he'd been totally in love with."

Heart. Stab. Turn of the knife.

She forgave Josie for that, since the young woman was *so* young and really going through some heavy growing pains right now. She was trying to be her own woman while being given a really hard time by her brick wall of a brother. Sometimes standing up for what you believed in the face of an adversary made you only more resolute, more sure, since you had to defend yourself. Sometimes people gave in. She admired Josie's strength.

"And everything he did for me alone—I could write a book," Josie continued. "When I was in high school, junior year, this pack of girls started being really nasty to me, starting rumors about my sexual preferences, that kind of thing. James marched into the principal's office the first time I mentioned I was having trouble. And he went every day until the girls were dealt with. He threatened to bring the media with him, and suddenly, no one wrote things on my locker anymore or whispered crap at me in the halls."

"Wow. That 'too much' you were talking about comes in handy sometimes."

"Yeah. It does," Josie said. "Which is why I feel so bad now about how things are between us. And what I just told you? That's just one thing, one-quarter of a year. When I think of everything else, and with my brothers and sisters added in too, I don't know how he did it. He deserves the world. He really does."

Ginger froze. How many times had she thought that same thing—he deserved the world, glad he was going to get it on his global summer trip. But here she'd been, hoping to get him to change his mind, his views of parenthood. She'd spent an entire evening trying to make him see that playing house with their little charge, Gia, would be wonderful. Instead, it had been…realistic. And she'd had the nerve to feel down in the dumps that her big plans for that night hadn't gone the way she'd hoped.

How flipping selfish could she be? Did she care about this guy? Or did she care only about what *she* wanted?

That was it.

She was letting him go. No more flirting, no more kissing, no more hoping.

Because if she really loved him, how could she keep trying to make him want something he so clearly didn't? How could she even *try* to deny James the chance to finally leave town, to see the world, to live responsibility-free for the summer?

She'd been so focused on herself and her needs that she really hadn't thought about him at all. And that was wrong. A good person, the person she wanted to be, wouldn't be trying to make him think playing house was what he really wanted when it wasn't. When he'd told her, in ways that had made her ache for him and all he'd been through with his siblings, exactly why he wasn't ready or interested in fatherhood.

And being a good person was why she'd come to town. Because being a good mother was all she cared about.

A light bulb pinged on above her head. Holy cannoli, she thought.

Being a good mother. It was never about how she looked. It was never about attracting a certain kind of man.

How could she have possibly missed such a simple truth?

Being a good mother was about *being* a good mother—not looking like a good mother. Being a good mother was about love, commitment, devotion, care, protection, values and showing up, every minute of every day.

Everyone learned in preschool that what was on the inside was what truly mattered—not the outside. Ginger had thought she'd understood that, that transforming on the outside was only a means to an end: looking the part to be safe from Alden, to find the right guy to be her baby's father. But honestly, did she want someone who'd judge the old her? Who'd make assumptions about her based on how skimpily she dressed? Because she'd flashed her cleavage all over the place? *That* made her a lowlife?

Alden, in his expensive suit, was the lowlife.

She shook her head, finally getting it.

And she knew exactly what she had to do in order to set James free. Time to call in the old Ginger.

Chapter Eleven

James insisted that Ginger take the next couple of days off from work. After getting her to promise she'd do nothing but lie in bed and read magazines and her baby books, including not attending class at the school, he felt a little better. She'd been pushing hard, and between all the internal pressure and starting a new job that had turned into something bigger, and all the stuff going on between them, she'd clearly had some kind of anxiety attack. He thought anyway. Amelia and Merry had reported that she'd been resting, and that Larilla had informed Ginger that she'd conducted herself with a little too much poise during her scare; if there were a next time, Larilla had said, Ginger was to scream at the top of her lungs for help.

Today she was due in for a half day at James Gallagher Solutions, and to be honest, he couldn't wait to see her. He'd missed everything about her.

He heard the front door open and close and the click of heels on the wood floor. And he was well aware of his heart rate speeding up, his excitement at seeing her. But when he casually strolled out, he almost didn't recognize her.

She wore one of her old favorite outfits. A barely there leopard-print miniskirt in some stretchy material. High-heeled sandals. The *babe* tank top showing a lot of skin and cleavage. Lots of face makeup and eyelashes so long they almost reached her eyebrows. And very red lips.

"Hiya!" she said.

He stared at her, then realized he shouldn't stare and tried to look away, but he couldn't. "Uh, hi?"

"Something wrong?" she asked, walking around her desk and sitting down, crossing her very long legs. He now also knew that her underwear was shiny and purple.

"Just surprised."

She blew a bubble and stuck her finger in it to pop it. Then she giggled. "Oopsies, hardly professional." She plucked the gum from her mouth and dropped it in the wastepaper basket under her desk. "Well, lots of work to do. I have at least ten calls to make this morning to follow up on clients before you leave on your trip."

"Ginger, what the hell is going on? Why did you... revert back?"

"Because this is really who I am, James. Plain and simple. And to be honest, the most important thing I learned from Madame Davenport is that being yourself is everything."

He stared at her. Dumbfounded. "I suppose it is. I just thought—"

Never mind. Perhaps this was all part of the process of "finding herself," being the woman she wanted to be. Sometimes you had to take a step back to go forward.

Not that this was a step back. Not really. Because as James stood there, trying not to stare at Ginger in her crazy getup, he knew, beyond a shadow of a doubt, that he had some very strong feelings for this woman. Her clothing was beside the point. Or maybe the clothing was the point. He liked her this way; this was who she was. As was her more professional look. It was all Ginger, all part of the whole.

He liked her as she was. However she was.

So there was only one thing to do with this new information. Avoid, ignore, make himself scarce.

"Well, we both have work to do, so…" With that, he awkwardly marched to his office and closed the door, his heart beating five miles a minute.

In no time at all, Ginger O'Leary had gotten so far inside him that she had him all tangled up.

There was a knock on the door.

He cleared his throat. "Come in."

She opened the door, a trail of her old perfume, the sexy spicy one, hitting him full in the face, full everywhere. "Before we get all busy, could I get your opinion?"

"Sure," he said.

"Madame Davenport asked me the other day if I'd

like to be set up on a blind date with a wonderful young man she knows, and, of course, I said yes. And not for an assessment either. A real date. With a real candidate to be Bluebell's father. Isn't that awesome."

Was it hot in here? Had his collar shrunk?

"I thought—" He bit his tongue. It wasn't his business, right? If Ginger had come to the conclusion that this was her look, then this was her look. He saw past the pound of makeup and skimpy outfit to the woman underneath, so why wouldn't any other guy?

Crud.

"You wanted my opinion on something?" he asked, hearing his voice tighten.

"I was thinking for tonight's big date I'd wear all black and be super elegant, but do you think I should go with color instead?"

Was that a tattoo on her shoulder? He peered closer and yes—yes, it was. *Hot Stuff*, it said. That hadn't been there before, had it?

"I think whichever," he said. "You look good in everything." Which was the truth.

The old look tended to eclipse the real Ginger, so he wondered if that was all tonight's date would see. The itty-bitty clothes, the over-the-top cleavage, the super-done hair with the big precise waves. You could barely see her gorgeous hazel eyes with all that black lining them, all that heavy mascara.

Maybe her date would be unable to resist her. Or maybe he'd think she wasn't his type. Maybe he'd fall head over heels and carry Ginger off to the Wedlock Creek Chapel and they'd marry at midnight. Ginger would have her "quality" husband and Bluebell a "quality" father. Hand-picked by his own godmother.

His heart lurched. Bile squeezed his gut. How could be so torn up about Ginger finding love with another guy when that was the whole point? When that was supposedly what he wanted for her because he wouldn't be that guy himself.

So why couldn't he bear the thought of her with someone else?

Amelia and Merry did a double take when Ginger arrived back at Madame Davenport's School of Etiquette.

"So this is a surprise," Amelia said.

"Big surprise," Merry added. "I thought you really liked your new look."

"I do. A lot. In fact, I've felt more 'me' the past two weeks than my whole life." The realizations she'd come to, the streamlined look, the little bit of poise she'd managed to make part of herself. She did like the person she became—for the right reasons.

"So you look like this because...?" Amelia asked.

Should she tell them? They were James's sisters, so she really shouldn't talk about him behind his back. But then again, they were *her* friends, and part of her life here at the school.

Like Ginger could ever hold anything in anyway.

"I'm trying to unattract your brother," she admitted.

Two sets of pale brown eyes bugged out.

"Wait—is there something going between you and James?" Amelia asked.

"He's trying his best for there not to be. He likes

me—*that* way—but he doesn't want to. And he certainly doesn't want the life he'd get with me. Instant fatherhood. Family man. Life laid out for the next eighteen years—for forever, really. And I care too much about him to let him 'pick me' when he needs to be a carefree bachelor."

"Ah, I get it," Merry said. "You're trying to turn him off."

She nodded, then wrapped her arms around herself as a chill crept along her bones. She'd shut him out this morning. In the weeks she'd known him, they'd been so honest with each other, but showing up looking this way, not telling him why, felt like a big fat lie. And she didn't like lies between them.

"James deserves the summer world trip. He deserves the next ten years to be free of heavy responsibility to anyone but himself. He's given so much to others, and now it's his turn to live the life of the wild and free. He can party. He can date a zillion women. He can take off for Vegas at a moment's notice."

Merry chuckled. "You're talking about James."

"You say that only because he's been *unable* to do those things the past seven years," Ginger pointed out. "You guys have always come first."

"We know," Merry said, her tone so reverent that Ginger reached for her hand and gave it a squeeze.

"So I'm going to make sure that James unfalls for me," Ginger continued. "And I'm going to fall for someone else too. Larilla set me up on a date tonight. She knows how important it is to me to find a good father for my baby. So I'm sure he's a wonderful guy."

At this point, Ginger knew she'd be just fine on her own. A great mother. Her life was in order. She didn't need a man to round anything out or make anything better. Yes, it would be nice for Bluebell to have a great dad. But she didn't need to seek one out anymore; if she met someone organically, fine.

But that someone would have to be exactly like James. And there couldn't possibly be two James Gallaghers in the world.

Yes, she would do just fine on her own.

"I'm sure your date will be a total catch," Amelia said.

"Definitely," Merry added.

Ginger adored these two.

"Want to know something?" Amelia asked. "Now that I know you, I don't even see the makeup or tiny skirt while talking to you right now. It's like I don't even notice it. But when Larilla showed us a photo of you from the day you arrived at the school, that was all I saw."

"I think that's what happens when you really and truly *see* a person," Ginger said. "And I'm glad you do see me. No matter what I'm wearing or how much makeup is caked on my face. It means we're true-blue friends."

The sisters beamed. "Good luck on the date tonight," Merry said.

She had a good feeling about it. Larilla was a shrewd, smart cookie. If she handpicked this guy for her, he had to be someone special. At the least, she'd have a nice time. But the pressure was off.

Ginger had no idea how anyone could be more special than James, but that was the point of going on the date, wasn't it? To allow someone to be more special to her.

Tall order.

Ginger was getting ready for her date—dressed like the new her—when there was a knock on the door. She put her hairbrush on the dressing table and opened the door. Sandrine stood there, tears streaming down her cheeks.

Ginger pulled her into her arms for a hug. "Hey," she said, dashing away her friend's tears from the tops of her cheeks. "What happened?"

Sandrine sniffled and dropped down on the edge of Ginger's bed. "If you ever need a dentist, don't go to Landon Cole, DDS. Trust me, he's the worst!" She broke down in a fresh round of sobs.

Clearly Sandrine hadn't just come from a dentist's appointment gone horribly. Landon was her boss. The one she was in love with despite having proved his jackassery during her assessment at the Cowabunga Café.

"I gave him the benefit of the doubt," Sandrine explained, dabbing under her eyes with a tissue. "I figured he was just saying what he thought Madame Davenport might expect from an etiquette student. But today at work, as a patient left the examination room, he said, 'I've always wanted to have sex on the exam chair. You in?'"

Ginger's eyes bugged out. "You're kidding. Please be kidding."

She shook her head. "I wish I were. And I said, 'That's incredibly inappropriate.' And he said, 'Oh please, you've been after me since you started working for me. I see the way you look at me, the way you talk to me. You want it, so come and get it, baby. I'm done being the good guy.'"

"What a pig!" Ginger said. "How is that being done with being the good guy?"

"Meaning it turns out he's engaged and has been good by not cheating. He's revolting!"

Ginger shook her head, revolted. What an absolutely despicable human being. "So what happened?"

"I told him he was a disgusting pig and that what he did constitutes sexual harassment. You should have seen the fear on his smarmy face! I quit and stalked out."

"Good. And report him to Madame Davenport. He can't be on her list of 'suitable' men for practicums."

She sniffled again and nodded.

"I'm so sorry, Sandrine. You're a great person. He was a rotten egg, the clichéd wolf in dentist's clothing."

"Well, I guess it was a good lesson," Sandrine said. "Just because someone seems like a catch doesn't mean he is. And I admit I overlooked some red flags because he was so hot and a dentist. That's on me. I won't make that mistake again."

Ginger nodded. "When someone shows you who they are, believe them."

"Amen," Sandrine said. She lifted her chin and then popped up. "You know what? I feel much better. Why am I wasting my tears on that walking, talking pile of horse dung? No more!"

"Got that right," Ginger said. "And I'll be paying very close attention on my date tonight. Just like I thought Alden was all that and a bag of Doritos just because he looked great and wore expensive suits and threw twenties around. Well, he was lower than low. Everything that matters is *inside*."

Sandrine hugged her. "I'm so glad I met you. I hope we stay in touch after the class ends."

"Of course we will. We're good friends."

Sandrine beamed. "I hope your date is amazing."

Me too, Ginger thought. But then again, no big whoop if it wasn't. She really would do just fine on her own. The old Ginger didn't think she had what it took to be a good mother, let alone a single parent. She'd believed she needed a good father for her baby to ensure the best life for him or her. But what her baby needed most of all was love and a devoted mama. Ginger would lavish her child with all that and more. And she had her head on straight, a solid job, good friends and a world of possibilities at her feet.

She didn't *need* a father for Bluebell to make up for her own deficits. Now she truly understood that. She *wanted* Bluebell to have a great dad because Bluebell deserved a great dad. Period.

I'll be assessing you, *Mr. Supposedly Amazing*, she thought once Sandrine left and she was back in front of her dressing table.

Of course, it was hardly fair that he had such big shoes to fill, but once you'd experienced what a great man was all about, you couldn't ever go for less.

Esme padded in and jumped onto Ginger's bed, spinning around until she was satisfied with her spot.

"Isn't that right, Esme?" she asked the cat as she put on a little mascara.

Esme raised her front leg and began grooming herself, which Ginger took as a yes.

Chapter Twelve

Ginger's date was an attractive accountant named Tyler Witowsky. He was the nephew of a woman in Larilla's book club. Ginger had always been a big reader, and of course, any time someone saw her with a book, that person would always say, with a totally shocked expression, "You read?" Eye roll. Anyway, books were the first topic of conversation. Ginger listed the last five books she'd read, which included a biography of Supreme Court Justice Ruth Bader Ginsburg—amazing life—and a psychological thriller everyone had been talking about a few months back. And of course she'd mentioned the book she was reading now: *Your Baby's Development, Week by Week*.

"My aunt mentioned that you were expecting a baby," Tyler said, sitting across from her in Rustico's, an Italian restaurant in Wedlock Creek. "So things didn't work out with the baby's father, huh."

"Nope. But I've started over here in Wedlock Creek, and I feel really positive about the future for myself and the little one. I have a great job, great friends and now a great place to call home." Technically, she didn't have a home, but she would. She'd been checking out rentals and there were several options for two bedrooms and even very small houses a good distance from town that she might be able to even buy, thanks to her even better salary—including part-time over the summer while James was gone. She'd see.

"I'm impressed," he said, his gaze thoughtful on her. "I'll be honest and tell you that I can't have kids of my own. A few girlfriends have said thanks, but no, thanks after hearing that."

She shook her head. "That's awful. There are so many options for having children. Biology isn't everything."

He smiled. "Well, here's to options."

She smiled back, and they clinked their sparkling waters. "You were probably taken aback though, when your aunt brought up the idea of going on a blind date with a pregnant woman." Though now that she thought about it, he probably liked the idea because he couldn't have children of his own.

"Well, I'll be honest again. This isn't exactly a blind date for me. I saw you when you first came to town, so I knew who you were. I was in the Solero Sisters Bakery getting a cake for my parents' anniversary when you came in and ordered a muffin. Blueberry, I recall."

Wow. He even remembered her order? "Oh. I don't remember—I was so distracted by hoping Madame Davenport would take me on as a student that I barely noticed anything else before that."

Which was true. Still, though Tyler was certainly pleasant looking, if *she* were honest, she'd confess he was not the kind of guy she'd notice right off. Now that he was sitting across from her, she saw he had nice dark brown eyes, and even though his hairline was receding, she liked the chestnut color. Fine, he wasn't her type. But her type hadn't served her well. Now her type was quality human. That was all.

The waitress came over to take their orders. Ginger had a craving for pasta, something decadent and cream-laden, and ordered the fettuccine carbonara with chicken, prosciutto and peas. Tyler went for the Aegean pizza special, and they also got a starter of garlic knots, which Ginger was craving so bad she could wolf down the entire basket.

Did Tyler pull a Landon Cole, DDS, and scowl and gape at the carbfest of an order? No, he did not. In fact, he said her choices sounded really delicious and hoped they could share a bite or two of their dishes. She liked this guy more and more each minute.

Even if he wasn't James Gallagher.

"Haley loved prosciutto," Tyler said, glancing down at the table. His face fell, and unless she was mistaken, tears were glistening in his eyes.

Gulp. Haley must have been someone close to him who passed away. "I'd love to hear about her," Ginger said. "Were you very close?"

He sighed, and just then the waitress returned with their garlic knots. She immediately popped one into her mouth, then realized she probably should have been more ladylike and pulled it gently apart or taken a bite instead of stuffing her face. But hey, she was pregnant and hormonal and had serious cravings.

"She has the most gorgeous blue eyes," he said, taking a sip of his water.

Did he say *has*?

"Everyone who knew I was going on a date tonight told me not to talk about her or even bring her up, but come on, is that realistic? We only broke up six months ago."

Six months seemed like a reasonable amount of time to have moved on. But then again, Ginger had never been in love.

Well, before now. Before James. And since there was no "them," there was nothing to get over. It was like being in a perpetual state of…off-balance-hood. So Ginger was hardly one to be judging here.

"How long were you together?" she asked.

James pushed the basket of garlic knots away from him as though he'd lost his appetite. "A little over two years. I knew she was the one, but I guess she wasn't as sure. She said it wasn't only because of the kid thing, but I don't know… I proposed seven times."

"Seven times," she repeated. Poor guy.

"The seventh time she told me she was sorry, but she just wasn't in love with me and had to face the truth so we could both find our true loves. Of course, she didn't mention that she'd already found her true love at work."

"Sorry, Tyler. That must have been really hard."

"I didn't think I'd ever get over it. But every month it got a little easier, I guess. And then I saw you in the bakery that day you arrived in town, and for the first time, I felt something. Granted, it was pure lust, but it hit me hard. I felt like you woke me up."

She laughed, then tried to stop since he was being so earnest. "Not that that's funny. I just mean, me, inspiring lust. Pregnant, alone, showing way too much booty."

"Well, you cured me. I mean, I'm still not over Haley. But I can finally see sleeping with another woman."

"Me?" she blurted out.

"Well, not you *this* way. The old way. But I guess since you're at Larilla's school, you've evolved from that look."

"Sorry, but yes." This was insane. Just this morning she'd dressed like the old her to unattract someone. Little had she known she'd saved a man's life because of the skimpy, big-haired her.

"Well, even if I'm not really attracted to you," he said, "you're very easy to talk to. It's nice to know I can go on a date and open up."

"I hear you," she said as the waitress served their dishes.

She dug into her comfort food, heaping a hearty amount of fettuccine carbonara onto Tyler's plate. He did the same with his Aegean pizza. "Mmm, feta cheese," she said, savoring the bite.

"So even though this isn't a love match, I hope we can be friends," he said. "I can really use a friend."

"Me too. And I'll be honest too. I'm not over someone either. Someone I didn't even get to have in the first place."

"Love sucks."

"But it's great too." Now that she knew what love was. It *was* great. It was everything.

He nodded and then their mouths were too full of food to talk much. They chatted, laughed, nodded, shared more of their entrées, and by the time they left, Ginger felt a little more connected to the world, crazy as things were.

She slipped her arm through Tyler's as they walked down Main Street.

"Coffee?" he asked, gesturing at the shop across the street.

"I'd love some," she said. "Decaf, of course."

As they were heading to Coffee Zone, Ginger caught sight of Josie Gallagher, looking much like the old Ginger, practically running into a lounge on her three-inch black heels. The young woman did not look happy. She wondered what was up with that.

Until she saw James, a huge scowl on his handsome face, throwing open the door and going in after her.

Ginger instinctively removed her arm from Tyler's. Since their date had evolved and now they were buds, she didn't want to let her feelings for James boss her around right now. Besides, she knew without a doubt that Tyler would understand.

She wished she could run after him. Comfort him, help him, try to make things right between the siblings. James was good at solving problems—except the one concerning Josie. She wished he'd let her help him. But he'd made his feelings on that front clear.

Same with the two of them having a future. So she stayed put.

"Hey, everything okay? You look like you saw a ghost."

"Just that guy I was telling you about," she admitted.

"There should be a rule that if someone breaks your heart, they have to leave town immediately, never to be seen again instead of still able to walk around in your breathing space."

"Right? Unfortunately, my guy is also my boss, so I can forget that."

"Oh, that is complicated," he said. "There's no way I could handle that. You must be a very strong person, Ginger."

"Strongish," she said. "Come on. Let's go have that decaf iced latte and something decadent to share."

As they walked into Coffee Zone, she told herself to stop thinking about James or wondering what was going on in the lounge. If he and Josie were at each other's throats.

Forget him for tonight, she ordered herself. *It'll be good practice.*

As if she could forget James for two seconds.

James stood just inside the door of the Lizard Lounge, his heart pounding. He could barely breathe. He needed water. He needed to sit down.

"James? Are you all right?"

He slowly glanced to his left. His sister Josie stood

there, peering at him. Was it hot in here? A cold sweat broke out on the back of his neck.

"James, what's wrong?" she asked, concern raising her voice. She dragged over a chair and he dropped down into it.

What's wrong is that I just saw Ginger out with her future husband, Bluebell's future father.

This was crazy. He didn't want to marry Ginger. He didn't want to be a father. But he couldn't handle the idea of her with another man. Again, again, again, that didn't make sense. He cared about Ginger. She meant so much to him. He should want all the pieces of her life to come together. A great dad for her baby was the reason she was here in the first place.

"I'm fine," he muttered, getting control over his racing heart and labored breathing back. The effect Ginger had on him was insane.

She'd forgone the old look she'd adopted for the office that morning. Tonight she was in a sundress that showed off her lush curves. He didn't think he saw the *hot stuff* tattoo, though she had been across the street. Her honey-blond hair was sleek to her shoulders, the big, stiff waves gone.

Any guy would fall in love with Ginger no matter how she looked. Because she was special, and that's all there was to it.

Not that he was saying he was in love with her. He wasn't. He just…cared about her. Deeply.

He was so lost in his thoughts that he hadn't even noticed Josie had left and returned now with a glass of water.

"Drink this," she said. "You're losing your mind, and water has restorative properties."

He took the glass and guzzled it down.

Josie raised an eyebrow.

As he glanced around the lounge, he saw seedy-looking men sitting at small round tables. Two skimpily dressed dancers were on each side of the stage, set off by neon multicolored lights. "This is where you're performing?"

"Yes. It is. Everyone gets their start somewhere."

"Josie, you're up," someone called.

"Wish me luck," she said, put her hand on James's shoulder and hurried to the stage.

She got two wolf whistles and a tiny round of applause.

Music started somewhere offstage, and Josie began to sing an old Whitney Houston song he always liked. Wow, Josie had a nice voice. A good voice. Had he known that? Her voice was folksy and strong at the same time, with serious range. He looked around the room—even the waitresses had stopped to watch. She commanded attention.

Huh.

When she finished, he stood up and clapped and whistled, and Josie came over to him, surprise lighting her face. "Guess you liked my performance."

"I had no idea you could sing like that. Why didn't you tell me?"

Although, now that he thought about it, why hadn't he ever gone to see her sing since she'd left school? He hadn't because he'd been too stubborn about his way or the highway. He hadn't cared about whether she could sing or not; all he'd cared about was her going back to school where she belonged. Her voice had been beside the point.

Only to him.

But not anymore.

She rolled her eyes and shook her head, but she was smiling. "More like you don't listen, bruh."

He was beginning to get that through his head. "You're amazing. Really. There's so much depth and feeling in your voice. Were you even in chorus as a kid? I don't remember that."

"I never had any confidence in myself to join stuff until college," she said. "And since I did and realized this is what I want to do, there's no stopping me. You never know where you're gonna get discovered. Maybe even here."

"I discovered you here. Could be a record exec in here too."

She nodded and then laughed. "Probably not, but as I keep getting gigs and at bigger establishments, there probably will be."

"I still wish you'd go back to school, Josie. But a gift is a gift, and if focusing on it is what you want to do, I support you."

She gasped and wrapped her arms around him. "Good. Because I like having your support. And blessing. But listen, James, there's someone else you need to get your head right about."

"Huh? Who?"

She tilted her head and made a funny face at him. "Ginger."

"Ginger? There's nothing to get right. Or wrong. We're friends. That's it."

She gave him a very slow nod. "Sure, you are. You're not in love with her."

He could feel his face flame. And his chest constrict. "I'm not."

"Right. That's what I said."

He narrowed his eyes at his sister. "She's on a date tonight with her maybe future husband. Larilla set her up."

"Oh, I'm sure she did. Clever, that Larilla. Never does anything without good reason."

Right. And the good reason was that Ginger could find her Mr. Right. Even if Larilla suspected that James had a thing for Ginger, his godmother knew he was leaving town very soon and had no interest in fatherhood. "Meaning?" he asked anyway. In case there was more he wasn't getting through his thick skull.

Josie laughed. "For a smart guy, you can be really clueless about what's staring you in the face."

So there was more. He shook his head. This was ridiculous. There was not more. Larilla knew how he felt. So she set Ginger up with someone else so that she could fall for another guy, and James could have the immediate future he wanted. "I *know* why Larilla set her up."

"Okay," she said very frustratingly.

"Oh, so if you're so smart, Josie Gallagher, tell me why Ginger showed up to work this morning looking like the old her. When I saw her just now, she was back to her new look for the date, so what gives?"

"Really? You don't know?"

So everyone understood everything about Ginger but him, it seemed. "I asked, didn't I?"

"James, Ginger is clearly madly in love with you. And she knows you have feelings for her too—feelings you refuse to acknowledge or act on. And because she does love you, she's putting you first. She's trying to get you not to be attracted to her. So she went for the caked-on makeup, *babe* tank top and tiny leopard-print miniskirt again. She probably blew a bubble a time or two."

"She did, actually." Could what Josie said be true? Ginger loved him?

He knew she liked him, of course, and was romantically interested, but because he'd put the kibosh on that, and she'd seemed okay, he'd figured they'd gotten past it. But the word *love* was big. Huge. If she loved him, she'd get hurt. Because...

He didn't want a family. Not right now. Not yet. If things were different, he'd be all over Ginger O'Leary. But she was pregnant, and her life was about to become something he wanted to run far away from.

"I was talking to Amelia and Merry," Josie said, her voice turning more serious. "And we feel pretty awful that coming home to take care of us turned you into such a lone ranger."

"I loved raising you guys. Every minute of it, even when it was hard. And it was hard. The five of you mean everything to me."

"But now you're about to give up the woman you

love because you think you don't want a wife and child right now."

"I don't though, Josie. I *don't* want a wife and child right now."

"Why though?" she asked. "What is it you're running from? Loving someone? Being loved back? Having a baby wrap his fist around your pinky while gazing at you with big slate blue eyes? Cradling a baby and marveling at the circle of life, while the woman you're madly in love with is taking a much-needed nap upstairs? Then you switch? Sharing all the beautiful moments life has to offer with the person who makes your heart skip a beat?"

He stared at his sister, aware his mouth had fallen open at some point.

"Because *that's* what you're running from, James. When it comes to Ginger anyway. The *idea* of a family, of responsibility is what crushes you. So replace the concept with real people. Ginger and her baby. You might see it differently."

Her words were swirling around his brain, sentences appearing in block letters in his mind's eye, narration accompanying as the letters trailed into his ears to shout the meaning. He shook his head to the left and right, trying to dislodge that feeling of having cotton stuffed in his ears.

"I'm leaving for Paris in a week," he said. "And then I'm coming home and sowing my wild oats. Taking weeklong vacations to Vegas. Going skydiving. You can't skydive when you have a wife and baby."

She crossed her arms over her chest. "I don't think I've ever heard you say you want to go skydiving."

"Josie, you're up again," a guy with the clipboard called out.

"It's your life," she said, then kissed him on the cheek and headed for the stage.

He dropped back down in the chair. *Get ahold of yourself, man. Josie is young and idealistic. Of course she thinks this way. Everything is a fairy tale to her.*

Except that wasn't really true. Her life had hardly been a fairy tale. His either.

Ginger's either.

Luckily, Josie's gorgeous voice filled the room again, and he focused on her song, trying to blot out everything she'd said.

Because all she'd said couldn't be true either.

Chapter Thirteen

Ginger had a packed morning of classes—her final exams—at Madame Davenport's today, so she wasn't scheduled to work. Good thing too. She'd have to dress up like her old self to turn off James, and she'd moved on from that woman. A woman who hid instead of revealed. A woman who was afraid to be herself. Last night, when she'd gotten back to the Queen Anne after her date with Tyler, she, Sandrine and Karly had holed up in Sandrine's room to study for their finals, which would include a not-multiple-choice test and a practical assessment—in the parlor at a cocktail party. Madame, along with the Gallagher sisters, would be watching, listening and rating her newfound skills.

Last night, on the porch, Tyler had asked if he could kiss her good-night, to see if there was anything there, and Ginger's heart broke for the poor guy. He was so miserable. She knew what that was like, so she'd said sure, and he'd puckered up and moved his face so slowly to hers that she took over and planted on one him—closed lipped, of course.

"Anything?" she'd asked.

"Your lips are soft," he said. "And you smell nice. But no."

"Aww, Tyler, you're just not ready. No need to rush it."

The good news on that front was that she and Tyler had decided to be true buddies, to help each other through these tough times of the heart. They were meeting for coffee at 7:00 p.m. tonight to celebrate the very good news that Ginger had a lead on a home for herself and Bluebell, and would finally be able to outfit a nursery. It turned out that Antonia Solero's aunt had a two-family house not too far from town, and though the available apartment was just a small two-bedroom, it would probably do just fine, and apparently, the aunt loved to cook big Italian dinners and invite everyone she knew. Ginger had called Lora Solero and had an appointment to see the apartment tomorrow morning.

By noon, the written exam was over, and Madame Davenport called Ginger into her office. She remembered sitting here three weeks ago well, scared, nervous, no idea how to be the person she wanted to be.

Ha. What she'd learned most at Madame Davenport's School of Etiquette was that she'd been that person all along. She just hadn't known it.

Madame Davenport handed Ginger her graded exam

across the desk, and Ginger's heart leaped at the grades on each. She'd gotten an A- on the place-setting section, but hey, who the hell could remember which spoon went first or which direction to place the knife? She'd gotten full As on the other two parts.

"I'm so proud of you, Ginger. And you must be very proud of yourself," Madame Davenport said. "You've come into your own."

She wanted to say, *I have, haven't I?* But a woman of dignity was more gracious in accepting a compliment. "Thank you, Madame. I've appreciated everything you've done for me."

Madame beamed. "And if I may ask…how did your date with Tyler go?"

"We've decided to become friends. We both have to get over other people, so we've decided to get through that together."

Madame sat back in her stately chair. "Ah, I thought he was ready. Sorry about that. And James is a stubborn one."

Ginger narrowed her eyes with a smile. "How did you know I was talking about James?"

"Oh, I was very sure the two of you were meant to be," Madame said, neatening the pile of papers in front of her. "From the get-go."

Ginger popped up straight. "What? What do you mean?"

"I know James—very well. And you showed me who you were immediately. I just had a feeling. And I was right."

"Right? But we're not together. We were never together.

He's leaving for the summer soon, and when he comes back, he'll be even further on his path to bachelorhood for at least ten years."

"He hasn't left yet," Madame said, straightening the piles on her desk again despite them already being very tidy. "Sometimes you have to put people together for different reasons. Like you and Tyler. There's a reason for most things."

Ginger narrowed her gaze again. "You're being rather cryptic."

"I have a lot of faith in the heart," Madame Davenport said. "And things falling into place."

But... "Are you saying I belong with Tyler in the end?"

Madame's expression gave nothing away. "Only you can decide who you belong with, my dear." She consulted her electronic tablet. "Your cocktail party assessment will be at 6:00 p.m. Good luck, Miss O'Leary."

And with that she was asked to please send in Sandrine.

So Madame had worked behind the scenes to put her and James together, despite her knowing how James felt. That seemed odd. And unlike Larilla Davenport.

Unless...she truly believed there was hope? That regardless of what James thought he wanted, they belonged together? A man who didn't want kids for ten years, and a woman about to have a baby?

Please. There was no hope.

And there certainly wasn't any hope with Tyler—not that she wanted there to be. So what was up with that?

For lunch, Ginger, Sandrine and Karly went to the

Pie Diner for their amazing potpies. They were celebrating good news—Karly had gotten her promotion to assistant editor at the *Wedlock Creek Gazette*, and Sandrine was feeling very empowered at having quit her job, especially because she'd gotten an even better job as a hygienist at a bigger practice with a big increase in salary. Ginger might not have something to celebrate, but at least she had the lead on the apartment and a new friend.

At five, Ginger was in her room getting ready for the cocktail party assessment, having no idea what to expect. Madame wasn't forthcoming about the guest list. Would James be there? Tyler? Her classmates? She really didn't know.

She wore the new emerald green sheath dress she'd bought the other day at Jazzy's. The saleswoman had been right about how the dress could go from work to an evening event. Different jewelry, different shoes, and voilà, a different look. Ginger hadn't had a clue about any of this stuff three weeks ago. Back then, her evening look was about adding ten more coats of mascara.

She glanced around her room at the etiquette school. She didn't want to leave here. Madame had new students arriving on the first of the month, so she had until then, but that was less than two weeks away. Hopefully Lora Solero's apartment would work out.

Ginger gave herself a final once-over, declared herself cocktail-party-assessment-worthy and headed down the gorgeous curved staircase. She'd miss this descent. She'd miss the oil paintings lining the walls, and the gorgeous old rugs. When she stepped into the front parlor, there were several groups of people chatting by the wall of bookcases, and another four or five people mingling by the floor-to-ceiling bay window, where a waiter wove through with a tray of appetizers. Another waiter held a tray of sparkling water and wine.

Ginger didn't know a soul here. How was that possible? Well, except for Amelia and Merry, but they were deep in conversation with someone else.

"All alone tonight?" a man asked, taking two glasses of white wine from a passing waiter's tray. "You look like you need this," he added, foisting one of the glasses on her. "God, I hate these parties, don't you?"

Ginger put the glass down on the little table beside the sofa. The guy was early thirties, okay-looking, with great blond hair. "Actually, I love parties. Chatting, meeting new people, seeing friends, the delicious little hors d'oeuvres." As a waiter passed with sparkling water, she took one of those.

"You don't drink? I couldn't get through one of these snoozefests without booze." He chuckled as though that were hilarious.

"I don't drink because I'm pregnant," she said, patting her tummy. "Just beginning to show."

"Oh," he said. "I didn't see a ring." His gaze slid to her left hand.

The last time she thought someone was being judgy about her lack of wedding ring, she was wrong, so she decided to give the guy the benefit of the doubt. Though he sure as hell was being rude. "No ring. I'm on my own."

"You should buy yourself a cheap gold band so people don't think you're—oh, you know," he said with a laugh and took a sip of his wine.

She narrowed her eyes. "That I'm what?"

"Going to be a single mother," he mock-whispered as though that were disgraceful. "The bigger you get, the more visible that ringless finger will look. It's like announcing to the world that you got pregnant and who knows what happened to the father."

Who the hell did this schmuck think he was? "Well, my story is my truth," she said. "I don't feel ashamed, if that's what you were getting at. Oh, I see someone I need to say hello to. Enjoy the party."

She rushed off as fast as she could, her heart pounding. What a horror show. Who did Larilla invite to this shindig? She moved over to an empty spot by the bookcase, glad she didn't actually recognize anyone. She needed to catch her breath.

"Hello," a woman said. "I don't think we've met. I'm Bea Blauman. The town librarian." She gave Ginger a warm smile and extended her hand.

Ginger shook it. "How nice to meet you. I'm Ginger O'Leary. I love to read. I've been busy with school and a new job, but I intend to stay put in Wedlock Creek so expect to see me in the library a lot. Can't wait to get my library card."

Bea smiled. "Great." She listed the library's hours, including the two days a week it was open till eight at night. "See you soon, then. Lovely meeting you, Ginger."

As the woman moved on, Ginger hoped there'd be more like her and fewer like the idiot with the good hair and awful conversation skills. Talk about an etiquette fail.

"Well, I must say, you certainly clean up well," someone said.

Ginger turned to find a woman sizing her up. Um, okay. What now? Ginger tried to place her, wondering if she knew her from around town, but she was pretty sure she'd never seen the woman before. She was around forty, with a strawberry blond bob and bangs, and red-framed eyeglasses. Ginger would definitely recall the glasses, so she doubted she'd run into this lady before.

"I remember when you first showed up in town," the woman continued. "It's quite amazing that a person can go from so—" she leaned closer and lowered her voice "—so *trashy* to this. I mean, excuse my French, but…" She looked her up and down, then leaned close again. "You seriously looked like a hooker. It really is a testament to Larilla Davenport that you changed to this degree."

No, it's a testament to Larilla Davenport that you're still standing, lady. Ginger wanted to take the mini mushroom quiche from the little plate in the woman's hands and fling it in her face. But she refrained. "My name is Ginger O'Leary," she said, extending her hand. The woman looked surprised, but shook it and introduced herself as Megan Nally. "I think it's quite unkind to refer to anyone as trashy or looking like a hooker. Makeup and clothing don't define a person. I'm the same woman I was three weeks ago."

"Oh please," Megan said, waving her hand. She snagged a smoked salmon cake, which looked delicious, and popped it into her mouth in one bite. "Clothes make the man. And the woman. Everyone knows that. You looked like a real you-know-what before."

"I don't know what," Ginger said through gritted teeth, though she tried to adopt a pleasant expression. "But you'll have to excuse me. Enjoy the party."

With that she slipped away, reining in her anger until she could get outside. How dare that horrid, judgmental woman! Ginger breathed in the lovely evening air and counted to five.

Oh, who the hell cares what some stranger thinks. I know who I am.

"A plus," a voice announced from behind.

Ginger turned around. Madame Davenport, the beyond-rude blond guy, and überjudgy Megan Nally stood there, all lightly clapping.

What was going on?

Ohhhh. The light bulb pinged on over her head.

"That was a test? How awful!" Ginger mock-scrunched up her face. She really should have anticipated it, but she thought tonight would be more about mingling and making appropriate small talk. Which she supposed she had.

"All the cocktail party assessments are individualized for the student based on her most burning questions," Madame Davenport said. "Yours had been about what to do when someone insults you to the point that you want to throw a scone at them. You asked how to handle that multiple times. It was your burning question because it brought together two areas that were getting the better of you in difficult situations—pride and impulsivity. However, you knew exactly how to handle yourself with rude party guests. You correct the other's bad behavior while remaining in control, and then you simply walk away. You even went the step further of politely *excusing* yourself, which earned you the plus."

Huh. *I think it's quite unkind to refer to someone as trashy... Clothes and makeup don't define...*

She had done that. And she had walked away. Politely. When she'd felt like dumping a platter of mini empanadas on Megan Nally's head.

She thought she hadn't changed all that much, but of course she had. In the best ways.

"Wow, that Megan lady is lucky you didn't punch her lights out," Tyler said as he and Ginger walked down the clothing aisle at BabyLand. They'd met for coffee after the cocktail party assessment, and Tyler had broken down in tears again in line because the woman in front of them ordered a skinny, no whip, iced Americano, which was his ex's exact order. Hey, sometimes the smallest things could trigger the biggest emotions.

Ginger had suggested they skip the coffee and go somewhere else, somewhere that wouldn't remind him of whatshername, but every place Ginger mentioned had him tearing up again until she'd mentioned offhandedly that she had to make a mental note to schedule a morning at BabyLand to start thinking about how she'd outfit her nursery. Now she had a steady paycheck—and a good one too—and hopefully by tomorrow, her own place to put a crib.

"Perfect," Tyler said. "My ex had no interest in motherhood yet, so being at a baby store won't remind me of her. In fact, nothing will trigger any memories there."

Which was how she'd ended up in BabyLand at 7:15 p.m. with Tyler Witowsky, holding on to her store-generated list of must-haves and her own little "registry adder," a little clicky device that allowed her to point and click at any item she wanted to add to her registry or wish list. That gorgeous white sleigh crib—on the list. Adorable lemon yellow sheets with tiny moons and stars—hers to be. A mobile, changing table and pad, all the necessities for diaper changing, for that matter, including that delicious-smelling baby lotion.

"Huh, I guess this is more boring than I thought," Tyler said with a grin.

Ginger conked him on the shoulder with a stuffed monkey, then zapped it with her registry adder. "Must-have."

She turned at the sound of sniffling. Oh God. Tyler was crying again.

"I thought nothing here could trigger you," she said gently. "What happened?"

"My ex wanted a pet monkey. Like on that old show *Friends*? Remember? Ross's monkey, Marcel? We watched all the seasons together. It was our thing." He broke down in a fresh round of sobs.

Oh brother. Ty sure was a crier. She shoved the monkey behind a bigger stuffed dolphin. "Let it out," she told him, drawing him into a hug. "Cry it out—it's the best way to heal. You're dealing with your sad feelings and that's the key."

She heard a sniffle, and felt him reach up to dab

under his eyes. He put his head on her shoulder. "I'm really glad we're friends, Ginger. You're great."

"Aww, thanks," she said, patting his back and giving him a big squeeze.

The sound of something thudding to the floor made her turn around. Oh God.

Standing there, with an entire display of stuffed globes at his feet, was, inexplicably James Gallagher.

Why he would be at BabyLand, particularly right before closing, was beyond her. But so was speech at the moment. Her breath caught in her throat, and she couldn't get words out, which was a good thing, since all she could think was, *Dammit, you look so good*. His blue shirt was almost the same color as his eyes, and he wore her favorite sexy jeans, the faded Levi's that molded to his incredibly sexy body.

He grabbed a bunch of globes in his arms and muttered a "Sorry" to the salesclerk standing nearby. The woman chased after a few errant globes that had made their way under displays.

Ginger headed over to help pick up the ones around James's feet. "How fitting is this?" she asked. "You literally have the world at your feet." She tossed a stuffed blue globe in the air and caught it. She closed her eyes and touched her finger to a random spot on the plush globe, then opened her eyes. "I landed on Brazil. Going there?" she asked.

Holy moly, she was losing her mind. This was the rambling nattering of a person who was completely off guard.

The fog cleared somewhat. "Forget all that," she said. "What in the world are you doing here?"

"What in the world—is that a pun?" he asked, no mirth in his voice as he practically tripped over a globe just behind his foot.

She shook her head. "Actually no. What *are* you doing here?"

"James Gallagher Solutions received an invitation to Antonia Solero's baby shower. Geneva's throwing it at the bakery. It's right before I leave. So I thought I'd pick up a gift from us before I get too crazy with settling up and packing."

"I see," she said. "You could have asked me to pick up a gift. I would have."

"Well, you're, um…" He coughed and glanced up the aisle, where Tyler was standing there with the stuffed monkey, staring at it as if willing himself to be immune to it. So far, no tears. "Busy," he finally said. "I happened to see you two on Main Street last night. I guess the date went very, very well."

Oh my God. He thought—

Do. Not. Correct. Him. She was back in her new Ginger look, which she knew appealed to him. So if he thought she and her blind date last night had hit it off to the point that they were still on the date in a baby store? All the better for James. Because he did care so much about her, James needed to think she'd found her man, her father for Bluebell, and that was exactly what he *must* be thinking right now. He could sail off for the independent, no-responsibility, no-wife-or-baby seas secure in the knowledge that she was A-OK.

Do not burst into tears, she sent telepathically to Tyler. *You'll give me away!*

"We really hit it off," she said, tossing a smile at Tyler, who was still staring very seriously at the stuffed monkey. James probably thought the guy took stuffed animal purchasing very seriously. Which was a good thing in someone she was passing off as Bluebell's future father.

She sighed inwardly at how silly and unnecessary all this was. Yet how *necessary* at the same time. She loved James with all her heart. And because she did, she had to let him live the life he really wanted, the life he deserved after all he'd sacrificed.

"Well, I'll let you two get back to your shopping," he said, grabbing a stuffed globe the salesclerk had missed and tossing it back on the display. He eyed Tyler, then her, and then beat the ole hasty retreat.

Taking her heart with him.

James left BabyLand without a gift for Antonia Solero. As if he could think straight, let alone choose a suitable shower gift for a client. He practically staggered outside, his hands clammy and a buzzing sound in his head.

He'd seen them embracing with his own eyes. They were now a couple. Ginger had found someone she liked—clearly a lot. And from the intense way the guy had been focused on that stuffed monkey in his hands, he took the buying of stuffed animals very seriously. That had to be a good thing. And since Larilla had set her up—he was pretty sure he was the something or other of someone from her book group—the man had to be a good guy. Larilla would have had him vetted. She liked Ginger that much.

Crud. So did he. He more than liked her and knew it, but every time the word *love* poked its way into his consciousness, he punched it away. You could love someone who, say, wanted to move to New York City when you were not a city guy, and there you had it—not gonna work. Unless one of you gave up your true nature. Not that living in a city or not was the best example for what was keeping him and Ginger from being a couple.

He'd never have the freedom he craved if he was with Ginger.

He'd never be able to just pack up and go. Spend a weekend in Vegas. Go mountain climbing in Utah. Get rip-roaring drunk with his college friends. Not that he saw them much anyway.

And not that he necessarily wanted to do any of those things. It was just that he hadn't been able to do anything these past seven years.

But Ginger with another man? The thought made him seriously sick to his stomach.

He stalked to his car and drove around for a while, wondering if they were still in BabyLand, picking out baby socks for Bluebell. He drove home, glad to discover none of his sisters were around. One look at him, and they'd interrogate him to find out what was bothering him.

What he couldn't understand was why the idea of Ginger with someone else bothered him so much. A quality father for her baby was the whole reason she'd come to Wedlock Creek and gone through the three-week etiquette course. To become a woman who'd attract the kind of man she wanted for Bluebell's dad.

He let out the sigh of all sighs as another thought began inching its way into his consciousness. He tried to bat it back, but it kept coming.

You already feel like Bluebell's father.

He shook his head, trying to dislodge the string of words flying past his mind's eye as if hung from an airplane. Of course he felt like the dad. He'd gone to Ginger's prenatal checkup and had seen Bluebell on the monitor. Heard the heartbeat. He'd been by Ginger's side through some ups and downs these past weeks. He felt a real sense of responsibility toward Ginger—that had to be the reason why he was having these feelings.

He found himself heading into the basement of his house—he made rare trips downstairs unless he really had to find something—and stared at the old trunks and luggage lining the back area. His parents' old trunks. His stepmother's luggage. All filled with things he and the quints hadn't been able to donate or have within view, like the brown leather jacket their dad had worn more than ten years or his mother's yellow Crocs that she wore for her favorite hobby, gardening in the backyard of the small house she'd rented when his dad had left. Kerry, his stepmother, had a ton of clothes and jewelry that the girls had gone through, keeping what meant something but unable to part with any of it, so down to the basement it all went. There were family photos upstairs, but not many.

He knelt in front of one of his father's chests and

opened it up. His dad's favorite clothes. The leather jacket. A few baseball caps he always wore on weekends. He opened another and found a bunch of the quints' old school stuff. Awards and binders full of math and writing assignments. Report cards.

In his mother's trunks he found more of the same, but from his childhood, which made him smile. Underneath his mother's yellow rain slicker he found a treasure trove of baby stuff. Pajamas and blankets and burp cloths that were sparkling white. She must have put this stuff away when he hit kindergarten. Surely Ginger could use all this. He wanted her to have it. He didn't open his stepmother's suitcases since he didn't feel right about it without the quints there, but he knew she'd put away their baby stuff. He opened up some of his own trunks and forgot half the things he'd put inside—Amelia's hospital bracelet from when she'd broken her leg and wrist. Eli's creative writing award from eighth grade, even though most of the stuff he'd written had been pretty dreary. Birthday and Christmas cards over the years.

There was one trunk full of stuff from the time he'd moved back home to take care of them until they'd graduated from high school. Awards and trophies and report cards and old stuffed animals. He took out the five matching teddy bears, all bedraggled and missing various body parts, an ear off one, a nose from another. He'd given the teddy bears to the quints for their second birthday when he was nine, with money he'd saved from his own birthdays and Christmases. They'd loved those teddy bears, loved that they were all the same, though he remembered the saleslady in the store telling him and his dad that maybe he should buy different ones so that each toddler would know his or her teddy. But nope, James knew they'd all want the same exact one—a family of bears.

The day he'd told the quints that their parents were gone, he'd found Merry in a closet with her bear, just holding it to her chest, tear streaks on her cheeks, her eyes red rimmed. He'd sat with her for a while in the closet, Merry silent except for when a sob would erupt from her throat. He'd been so scared—in general—of letting them down, but something occurred to him just now. He hadn't been scared in that closet. It was his job to be there for Merry, for their siblings, and he slipped into the role kind of effortlessly; he wasn't sure how or why. There'd been no strain on his part. Caring for them required organizational skill and patience, two traits he had in abundance.

He always thought of raising the quints as a sacrifice, but he hadn't sacrificed anything. He'd just been himself. The James Gallagher he'd been and was meant to be.

He'd raised the quints out of love, not obligation.

"James? You down there?" called Amelia's voice.

He stood up. "Yup. Just looking at some old stuff."

"Why?" she asked as she came down, Merry behind her. "What were you looking for?"

"Nothing. I just got nostalgic, I guess. I found some of my old baby clothes and thought Ginger might want them. There's a bunch of newborn-size pj's."

"You should definitely give them to her," Amelia said. "Our old stuff too."

He nodded. "I'm sure she'll appreciate that."

"Did you hear Ginger passed her exams with high honors?" Amelia added. "She got an A plus on her cocktail party assessment."

"Well, that doesn't surprise me. Ginger is tops at everything."

His sisters looked at one another with devilish smiles. Oops. He opened himself up for questioning. And he was in no state to be asked questions about his feelings for her. Not when he just realized the truth. And the depth of the truth.

"Amelia, Merry," he said. "Let me ask you something. Are you two happy working for Larilla? I mean, is that what you want to be doing?"

"Actually, we've been talking a lot about that," Merry said, dropping down on one of their dad's trunks. Amelia sat down on another, and James did too. "You know, when we were little, we thought Larilla's house was like a castle, and that she was some kind of fairy godmother from a storybook. We didn't get to spend much time at the school since Dad and Larilla couldn't exactly stand each other. But you'd bring us over when Larilla invited us to lunch and barbecues, stuff like that, and we were just enamored by her and the school. We wanted to be princesses, and we thought Larilla could turn us into Cinderellas."

Amelia laughed. "Of course, were we seven, eight, then. When we were teenagers, we got interested in the school and what Larilla taught because the school offered a 'Becoming a Strong Young Woman' work-shop, and we thought that was so cool. But then as we were graduating from college and you really pushed the school hard, wanting us to learn the business from Larilla, be in place to take it over, and it felt…pushed on us, you know?"

Merry nodded. "But now that we started really think-ing about what we want, we realize how happy we are at Larilla's, that we do love the etiquette business. We love how individual Larilla makes it. It's not one size fits all. She teaches based on the student. I think it's groundbreaking."

He was happy to hear this, but had they said they didn't want to work for Larilla and in fact wanted to pursue *x, y, z*, he would have been fine with that too. He didn't need other people's ducks to be in a row to feel his world was in order. He had to let his sisters be, just as his brothers had forced his hand at that by skip-ping town to pursue their dreams. Likely to get away from their controlling older bro. He'd visit both before he left town and make sure they knew how proud of them he was.

"It's weird to suddenly realize that the life you thought you didn't want was what you want after all," Merry said. "Like, if you have it, it must not be that great. Talk about spiting yourself, right?" She shook her head. "We love working for Madame Davenport's and we love Larilla. We couldn't be luckier actually."

He stared at Merry, the truth of what she'd just said slamming into his gut. Josie's words came back to him too.

What is it you're running from? Loving someone?

Being loved back? Having a baby wrap his fist around your pinky while gazing at you with big slate blue eyes? Cradling a baby and marveling at the circle of life, while the woman you're madly in love with is taking a much-needed nap upstairs? Then you switch? Sharing all the beautiful moments life has to offer with the person who makes your heart skip a beat?

Could turquoise waters and pink sand ever mean to him what Ginger did? Could eating insanely good pasta in Rome ever match a night at home with her?

Could dating other women ever really interest him when his heart was with Ginger and a baby he already loved as his own?

If he married Ginger, he'd marry her for love, not out of a sense of duty or obligation.

And he loved her so much that he ached, and he ached because he was in love with her.

He finally admitted it to himself. James loved her. All of her. Every bit of her. Including Bluebell.

Love was what mattered. And he loved Ginger O'Leary.

He just hoped he wasn't too late. For all he knew, her new boyfriend had carried her off to the Wedlock Creek wedding chapel.

Chapter Fourteen

Ginger sat at the desk in her room at Madame Davenport's, sketching a drawing of the layout of the apartment she'd just seen. Lora Solero's house was pretty far from town, which might not be a plus, especially when she was out of diapers or coffee. But the bedroom she'd designate as the nursery was light filled and had good vibes. She sketched in where she'd put the pretty white crib she'd zapped onto her registry at BabyLand, and then the dresser. The glider chair in a corner, and the moon and stars rug in the center.

She put her pencil down and studied the drawing, scrunching up her face. Something wasn't right, and she couldn't put her finger on it. Not with her plan for the layout, but the place itself. It was fine, perfectly okay and a good deal, but something was missing. And she had no idea what.

A knock came at the door. She hoped it was Karly, who had amazing drawing skills and maybe could re-arrange her ideas; maybe then the place would magically feel right to her.

But when she opened the door, it was James who stood there, looking very serious and somewhat out of breath, as if he'd run here from his house.

"Everything okay?" she asked, gesturing him in and closing the door behind him.

"No. Nothing is okay."

"What's not okay?" she asked slowly. She took his hand and pulled him inside, then shut the door behind him.

"That we're not together," he said. "That we're not a couple. I love you, Ginger, and I want to marry you and be Bluebell's father."

She gasped and staggered backward a couple steps. "What?"

"I've been an idiot and I'm rectifying that. We should be together. Paris and Machu Picchu don't matter as much as you do. Doing what I want doesn't matter as much as you do." He got down on one knee, a little black box in his hand.

Another gasp came flying from her throat.

"Will you marry me, Ginger O'Leary?"

She had to grab onto the desk chair with her right hand or her knees would have given out. James Gallagher had just proposed to her? *What?*

The man she loved so much, her dream come true—for herself and for Bluebell—had just asked him to marry her, on one knee, a diamond ring twinkling in velvet in his outstretched hand.

Which was why she had to say no. James's dream was *not* about marriage and family right now. But he always did the right thing, and acting out of love—and she did believe James loved her—didn't negate the fact that he was propelled to act out of that innate sense of responsibility. To her, it felt like him taking on the quints all over again. Of course he loved them, of course he'd give up his plans—for seven years to stay home to care for them.

But this time, there wasn't a teenager to be found. She was a grown woman who could take care of herself. She wasn't letting James give up anything for her. She loved him too much.

"Oh—I should add that I'd like to get married anywhere but the Wedlock Creek Chapel with its crazy legend of multiples," he said. "One baby sounds just right. The possibility of five? Maybe not right now." He smiled. "We could elope. Or have a big wedding right here in Larilla's garden. I know how you love walking through the garden. Or a church wedding. Whatever would make you happy, Ginger."

Ow, her heart. What would make her happy would be to scream *yes* at the top of her lungs and fling herself into his arms, seeing that gorgeous diamond ring on her finger.

And she wasn't about to argue with him over what he wanted. He'd insist that this *was* what he wanted to do—and she knew deep in his heart it wasn't. She had to let him go in a way that would have him on that plane to Paris. And there was only one way to do that.

"James, I appreciate the proposal—more than you'll ever know. But I can't marry you. I've fallen hard for Tyler—the guy with me in BabyLand yesterday—and I had no idea I could feel this way for a man. I'm so lucky that he's happy to take on an instant family."

The smile had long faded from James's handsome face. He snapped the ring box shut and stood up. "I'm too late, then. My own fault." He turned away for a moment as if collecting himself, then looked at her. "I wish you all the best, Ginger." With that, he fled from the room, and from the sound of his footsteps on the stairs, he'd taken them two at a time.

Ginger dropped down on the floor, her hands covering her face, and let the sobs come.

James had walked miles around Wedlock Creek, head down, hands shoved in his pockets. He didn't want to go home. He didn't want to drown his sorrows in pints of beer. He didn't want to do anything. So he just walked. The happy couples pouring out of the wedding chapel were unbearable, so he headed in the opposite direction down Main Street.

And stopped short.

Tyler, Ginger's new dude, was sitting at the bar of McCann's Pub, an elbow propping him up. The guy looked sad, like he might start crying at any second. If he hurt Ginger—

James found himself pulling open the door and

barging in, ready to confront Tyler. Though, given that he'd just come from her bedroom and she was perfectly fine and talking about how Tyler was The One, something else had to be wrong here. Maybe Tyler *intended* to hurt Ginger. Maybe he'd realized he'd taken on too much for himself.

Maybe this, maybe that. Stop speculating and talk to the guy.

Everyone else glanced over at him, since he pulled open the door with such force, but woebegone Tyler didn't even lift his downcast head. James pulled up a stool next to him. "Tyler, right? We, uh, ran into each other at the baby store yesterday. You were with Ginger."

Tyler turned toward him, then lifted his beer and slugged it down. "Oh, right. I always thought Haley was going to be the mother of the children we'd adopt, but I guess that's not happening." He shook his head. "I should just accept that I'm never getting over her."

"Over who?"

"Haley. My ex."

"But you're with Ginger now. You're buying stuffed monkeys for the baby."

"Huh?" he asked. "Ginger's awesome, but we're just friends. Want to know something pathetic? My friends were so sick of me whining and crying over Haley that I stopped and just kept it in. But Ginger encourages me to let it out. She's really great."

Okay, what was going on here? "So you and Ginger are *not* a couple. That's what you're saying?"

"Not in the slightest. Honestly, I found her a lot hotter before the big transformation. I told her too. I mean, she's pretty and all, but…"

Something that felt a lot like hope pinged in James's chest. Ginger had lied about them being a couple? Why? She'd said she'd fallen hard for Tyler. Maybe she'd fallen for Tyler but since he was still in love with his ex, he was the unattainable man? He frowned; that didn't feel right either. Ginger had definitely made it sound like James was her guy.

He got up and put a twenty on the bar. "Your tab's on me," he said. "And you will meet a woman who'll make you forget all about your ex. Trust me. I've been there and done that. I met someone so beautiful, so wonderful, so special, that I can't even remember my ex's name."

Until he said it, he hadn't even realized how true it was.

"Really? That gives me hope," Tyler said.

James clapped a hand on his shoulder. "Scout's honor."

He had to find Ginger right now. That was how bad he wanted his new life to start.

"Madame Davenport, I'll never have the words to thank you for everything you've done for me," Ginger said. "So I'll just have to say a simple thanks. You've changed my life."

Larilla stood up from behind the desk in her office and came around. Ginger stood up too. Madame Davenport pulled her into a hug. "*You* changed your life. From the very moment you decided to. I'll never forget meeting you for the first time, when you sat right there and told me your story."

Ginger glanced at the chair she'd just vacated. Could that have been only three weeks ago? It felt like three *years* ago.

"I'm certainly not afraid of Alden trying to take my baby from me anymore," Ginger said, sitting back down. "I doubt I'll ever hear from him again, but if I do, I'll handle it just fine. Not a single pastry will be thrown too." She laughed, then immediately burst into tears.

Oh no. No, no, no. She could not cry in front of Madame Davenport. But she couldn't get ahold of herself. Madame and James were so intertwined that just being with Larilla made her feel connected to James. Which made her cry harder.

"You were very honest with me from the very start," Madame said. "Please continue the tradition. What is wrong, my dear?" She took Ginger's hand and led her to the velvet chaise against the back wall.

Just like the first time she sat in this office, out came the whole story. Every bit of it. Starting with how respected James made her feel when he took her to that first boutique, to his accompanying her to her first prenatal checkup, to crying Tyler, to James's marriage proposal.

"I love him so much that I have to let him go," Ginger said, wiping at her eyes. "He deserves the world after all his sacrifice. But to have been so close to everything I've dreamed of and to give it up—wow, that hurts. But I'm okay. I'll be okay."

Larilla handed her a tissue. "Dear, at Madame Davenport's School of Etiquette, we don't expressly teach that one shouldn't make decisions for other people, but we should."

"But I'm not making a decision for James. I'm letting him have what he truly wants. His freedom."

"Oh? He proposed marriage to you and you turned him down because you think a wife and baby aren't what he truly wants. So you made that decision for him."

"Well, I…"

"Ginger, a wife and baby may not have been in James's plans. But you and your baby *are*. The concept of responsibility and caring for a family seemed like something he'd had enough of. But when faced with the reality of a *particular* pregnant woman, he chose the family. He chose you."

"Because he cares about me. Obligation is hardwired into him."

Larilla shook her head. "Nope. Love is. Want to know something, Ginger? Seven years ago, when James's father and stepmother died and he was left guardian of five grieving teenagers, I cared about him so much that I offered to take the quints in."

Ginger gasped. "I had no idea."

"He thanked me profusely and said he'd no doubt be leaning on me quite a bit. Then he said something I'll never forget."

"What did he say?" Ginger asked.

"He said, 'The quints are my heart.' And when he said that out loud, so definitively, something clicked for him. His fear about taking on such enormous responsibility became manageable. Because his priorities were in order, Ginger. First and foremost, above all else, the quints were his heart. So that won the day. And it was all that mattered."

"But—"

"No *buts*, Ginger. Madame Davenport's School of Etiquette would say the proper protocol in this situation is to speak to the gentleman in question." She smiled and took Ginger's hand, giving it a pat. "Go talk to James. And listen. Really listen to him."

Hadn't she herself told James when he needed to listen? Maybe now it was her turn to listen.

There was a knock at the door.

"Excuse me for a moment, dear," Larilla said, going to the door and opening it. The chaise was against the wall behind the door, so whoever it was wouldn't see Ginger's tear-streaked, puffy face.

"Larilla," she heard James say, "please tell me you know where Ginger is. I have to talk to her. It's urgent."

Larilla turned to Ginger and smiled, then back at James. "I know exactly where she is."

His relief—that she hadn't already fled town and changed her name, never to be found again—had James unable to speak or even catch his breath as he led Ginger upstairs to her room. She was right here, inches from him, and he was never letting her go again.

"So I ran into Tyler a bit earlier," he said as they went inside her room. Ginger shut the door behind them. "He was sitting in McCann's, drowning his sorrows at the bar. Boy, was I surprised when he started crying over a woman named Haley."

Ginger sat down on the edge of her bed. "I thought I had to let you go, James."

He sat down beside her and took her hands in his. "If I have to spend the next seventy years convincing you that I want this—you and me and Bluebell—I will. Because the two of you are everything, Ginger. You and Bluebell are my heart."

He could see tears glistening in her eyes. But she didn't say anything.

"I thought I wanted freedom, Ginger. But all I really want is you. And Bluebell." He untangled one of his hands and placed it on her belly. "This baby already feels like mine. I *am* Bluebell's father. There is nothing I'll ever want more than the two of you beside me."

She flung herself into his arms and he held her, one hand caressing her hair, the other keeping her against him.

"Does that mean you finally believe me?" he asked.

"Larilla talked some sense into me. So yes."

"Well, I did spend our entire relationship telling you I didn't want a wife and child for ten more years, so I get it." He reached up and touched her face. "I'm so sorry for how much I hurt you, Ginger."

"Eh," she said, waving a hand. "Old news. I'm sorry I lied about Tyler. I hope he's going to be okay. Poor guy."

"I told him I'd been there, done that until I met the woman of my dreams and now I can't even remember my ex's name. That perked him up."

"Whodathunk a month ago that Ginger O'Leary

would be the woman of James Gallagher's dreams?" she asked with a grin.

"You know who knew? Larilla Davenport, that's who. No doubt she saw this a mile away."

Ginger laughed. "Yeah, probably. She had you pegged. You liked me even when I had a face caked with makeup and tiny tops covered in rhinestones. You saw me, James. You always saw *me*."

He nodded. "And I love you. Very much. I always will, no matter what you look like."

"I love you too, James. With everything I am."

He pulled her against him again and held on to her. But then he realized he had a ring burning a hole in his pocket and a marriage proposal to remake.

He got up and dropped to one knee, holding out the open ring box. "Take two," he said. "Ginger O'Leary, will you do me the honor of becoming my wife?"

"Hell yeah, I will," she said with a grin.

He took the ring and slid it onto her finger. "I have a really good idea. Let's get married right away. Like, this weekend."

"In Larilla's garden," she said. "And a two-month honeymoon around the world sounds awesome. Bluebell can't wait to try paella in Spain and linguine in Rome and ramen in Japan and—"

"I was planning on staying put," he said. "I don't need to see the world when I have the world in you, Ginger."

"Are you *trying* to make my waterproof mascara streak down my face?" she asked, her eyes glistening with tears again. "Jeez. But, of course, you're going to see the world. Bluebell and I are coming with you. I even have a current passport. I always figured I'd use it someday."

Everything inside him felt lit and zinging like a pinball machine. "That would make me incredibly happy. And your doc will be okay with it? We can double-check before we start booking your tickets."

"James, I'm only three months along. We'll be long back before I'm on the be-careful track. So, world, here we come."

He grinned and kissed her. "So I get to see the world with the love of my life, then I get to come home and await the birth of our baby. Oh, and while we're waiting, we'll go house hunting for the perfect home for three of us. Sound good?"

"Sounds like a dream," she said. "It really does."

"To me too. How did I get so lucky?"

"Howdya like to get lucky right now?" she asked, giving her shoulders an exaggerated shimmy.

"You can take the girl out of the Ginger, but not the Ginger out of the girl," he said, whipping off his T-shirt.

"That makes absolutely no sense," she said on a laugh.

"As if I can think straight when I'm finally about to make love to my beautiful, sexy, amazing fiancée?" he commented as his jeans joined hers on the floor.

And then they were much too busy to talk any more.

Epilogue

The wedding wasn't that weekend. Not when Ginger ended up having so many bridesmaids who needed more than a few days' notice. So they'd waited until the following weekend, which worked even better because then they would leave for Paris the next day.

Ginger had asked her two close friends from Busty's—Desiree and Jilly—and her former manager, Coco, who'd hooked her up with Madame Davenport's School of Etiquette in the first place, to be bridesmaids. And Josie, Amelia and Merry, of course. And there was no way she wasn't asking Sandrine and Karly. She'd asked Madame to both be her maid of honor and give her away, and Larilla had tearfully accepted.

Now, with the ceremony just minutes away, Ginger looked at herself in the full-length floor mirror in the first-floor guest room, which had been turned into her bridal prep room. Her wedding gown was so beautiful that Ginger never wanted to take it off. Not even for her wedding night. But because it was to her ankles and very formfitting, there would be no way to *have* a wedding night with the gown on. The Gallagher sisters had gone bridal shopping with her, and they hit all the bridal shops in a three-hour radius. She'd found the dress of her dreams in a bridal shop in nearby Brewer. There it had been, hanging in the window. It was strapless white satin and very glam, with a row of beads at the empire waist. Simple but sexy. And now she would be wearing it to marry the man she loved.

Ginger's mother had once bought her a tiara as a gag gift when she was a teenager and getting a little princessy in attitude, and it was now her headpiece, so she had something old and her mama with her today.

"You look absolutely beautiful," Larilla said. "And it's exactly five o'clock. The procession is about to begin."

"We're ready," Amelia called from where the bridesmaids clustered at the door. The French doors to the garden were just across the hall.

Ginger glanced at Desiree and Jilly in their tiny, sexy blue dresses—that was the only bridal party directive—blue. Coco, who'd been beside herself with pride and happiness for what she'd had a part in making happen, wore a one-shouldered periwinkle gown with a thigh-high slit. Ginger loved seeing her old and new worlds commingling.

And then finally it was time. The wedding march

began, and Larilla took her arm and led her down the white-carpet aisle to where James stood under a gorgeous arbor that Larilla had had constructed for them. To his side were his groomsmen, which included his two brothers. Eli and Anders looked a lot alike, with the same sandy blond hair and pale brown eyes as their sisters had. James's high school and college friends rounded out the handsome lineup in their suits. According to Larilla, there was already lots of flirtation among the wedding party.

Ginger didn't have all that many people to invite—her bridesmaids were her crew, and that was about it. But all these people sitting on the white wooden chairs in Larilla's garden, from the community, would soon become part of her life. They were James's clients, old family friends and current friends. Tomorrow, she and James would be leaving on their world tour, and as he'd said, she already felt like she had the whole world right here.

As she passed Tyler on the aisle seat and gave him a smile, she noticed he had eyes for only one woman, standing alongside the stunning arbor: Jilly, her bridesmaid who worked at Busty's. No surprise there, given Jilly's teensy blue bandage dress, big hair and dangling rhinestone earrings to her bare shoulders. Jilly was a total sweetheart. Ginger grinned, thinking about how right those two might be for each other. Her former co-worker had recently gotten her heart smashed and had vowed to find a standup guy. And Tyler clearly had a thing for a certain look and was a good match for Jilly personality-wise. Jilly would steal his heart in no time. Then it would be "Haley who?"

Arms linked, Larilla led Ginger down the aisle to her waiting groom, and James looked so handsome in his tux that Ginger could have let out a wolf whistle. She didn't, but she wanted to.

You look incredibly beautiful, James mouthed to her.

You too, she mouthed back.

The minister spoke of love and commitment, of forever, and Ginger almost couldn't believe this wasn't a dream. She was really here, marrying the man she loved so much.

And then on this beautiful early-June afternoon, Ginger O'Leary married James Gallagher, Bluebell giving a little kick in celebration just as the minister announced it was time for the groom to kiss his bride.

* * * * *

Keep an eye out for Melissa Senate's next
Wyoming Multiples book,
available in July 2019!

And catch up on these previous books in the series:

The Baby Switch
Detective Barelli's Legendary Triplets
Wyoming Christmas Surprise

Available now from Harlequin Special Edition!

COMING NEXT MONTH FROM
H HARLEQUIN®
SPECIAL EDITION

Available April 16, 2019

#2689 A FORTUNATE ARRANGEMENT
The Fortunes of Texas: The Lost Fortunes
by Nancy Robards Thompson

After five years of working—and falling for—Austin Fortune, Felicity Schafer seems no closer to a promotion, or to getting Austin to open up. Will giving notice finally get Austin to *take* notice?

#2690 SWITCHED AT BIRTH
The Bravos of Valentine Bay • by Christine Rimmer

After finding out she was switched at birth, Madison Delaney heads to Valentine Bay to learn more about her birth family. She never expected to have feelings about Stren Larson, the shipbuilder who lives next door to her rental. But they come from such different worlds... Will they be able to see if those feelings can turn into forever?

#2691 HIS TEXAS RUNAWAY
Men of the West • by Stella Bagwell

Veterinarian Chandler Hollister has brought home many strays...but no one like lovely Roslyn DuBose. Exhausted, the single soon-to-be mom gratefully accepts his help. As one night becomes many days, Roslyn finds her way into Chandler's heart. But before this working man becomes a family man, Roslyn must face the one obstacle to their happy future: her secret past.

#2692 DOUBLE DUTY FOR THE COWBOY
Match Made in Haven • by Brenda Harlen

When Regan Channing finds herself pregnant, the last thing she expects is for another man to make her his wife! *Especially* not former bad boy Connor Neal. Pretty soon Regan's newborn twins have him wrapped around their fingers. But can the deputy's debt of obligation ever become true love?

#2693 THE CITY GIRL'S HOMECOMING
Furever Yours • by Kathy Douglass

Recent New York transplant Megan Jennings just found the ideal temporary home for sixteen suddenly displaced pets. Too bad the farm's owner isn't giving her the same warm welcome. A city girl broke Cade Battle's heart, and he refuses to trust the feelings Megan awakens. But Megan knows she's finally found her forever family. Can she make Cade believe it, too?

#2694 DEALMAKER, HEARTBREAKER
Wickham Falls Weddings • by Rochelle Alers

Big-city man Noah Wainwright has always viewed business as a game. But when he stumbles across bed-and-breakfast owner Viviana Remington, she's playing by different rules. Rules that bring the love-'em-and-leave-'em playboy to his knees... But when Viv learns how the Wainwright family plays the game, all bets are off.

YOU CAN FIND MORE INFORMATION ON UPCOMING HARLEQUIN® TITLES, FREE EXCERPTS AND MORE AT WWW.HARLEQUIN.COM.

HSECNM0419

Get 4 FREE REWARDS!

We'll send you 2 FREE Books plus 2 FREE Mystery Gifts.

AMERICAN HEROES

The Captains' Vegas Vows

Caro Carson

SPECIAL EDITION

Almost a Bravo

Christine Rimmer

Harlequin® Special Edition books feature heroines finding the balance between their work life and personal life on the way to finding true love.

FREE Value Over **$20**

SPECIAL EXCERPT FROM

HARLEQUIN®

SPECIAL EDITION

Big-city man Noah Wainwright has always viewed business as a game. When he stumbles across bed-and-breakfast owner Viviana Remington, she's playing by different rules. Rules that bring the love-'em-and-leave-'em playboy to his knees... But when Viv learns how the Wainwright family plays the game, all bets are off.

Read on for a sneak preview of Dealmaker, Heartbreaker, *the next great book in bestselling author Rochelle Alers's* Wickham Falls Weddings *miniseries.*

After the walk on the beach, she'd become overly polite and distant. Knowing he wasn't going to sleep, Noah sat up and tossed back the sheets. He found a pair of shorts and slipped them on. Barefoot, he unlocked the screen door and walked out into the night. He saw something out of the corner of his eye and spied someone sitting on the beach. A full moon lit up the night, and as he made his way down to the water, he couldn't stop smiling.

She glanced up at him and smiled. "It looks as if I'm not the only one who couldn't sleep."

Noah sank down next to her on the damp sand. Even in the eerie light, he could discern that the sun had darkened her skin to a deep mahogany. "I was never much of an insomniac before meeting you."

Viviana pulled her legs up to her chest and wrapped her arms around her knees. "I'm not going to accept blame for that."

"Can you accept that I'm falling in love with you?"

Her head turned toward him slowly, and she looked as if she was going to jump up and run away. "Please don't say that, Noah."

"And why shouldn't I say it, Viviana?"

"Because you don't know what you're saying. You don't know me, and I certainly don't know you."

Don't miss
Dealmaker, Heartbreaker *by Rochelle Alers,*
available May 2019 wherever
Harlequin® Special Edition books and ebooks are sold.

www.Harlequin.com

Looking for more satisfying love stories
with community and family at their core?

Check out **Harlequin® Special Edition**
and **Love Inspired®** books!

New books available every month!

CONNECT WITH US AT:

Facebook.com/groups/HarlequinConnection

**ROMANCE WHEN
YOU NEED IT**

HFGENRE2018